OF SUMMER AND WINTER

Angela L. Costello

This book is a work of fiction. Any and all references to historical events, persons, or locations are used as such in a fictitious manner. Names, characters, places, events, and likenesses are creations of the author and any resemblance to actual events, places, or persons living or dead, except those inspired by those acknowledged in this book, are completely coincidental.

ISBN: 1480083968
ISBN-13: 978-1480083967

Dedicated to those that live the dream, daily.

CONTENTS

ACKNOWLEDGMENTS

I wish to personally thank the following people for lending pieces of their own imagination to be part of my inspiration and other help in creating this book:

Pat, Dave, Matt, Jack, and other "staring" members of the 'Keep (If you're not in this one, you'll be in the next one, promise)

Jack, Crystal, Eli, Erik, and Dayna for being my beta readers

Max and Patrick for being my fact checkers

Kyla, who was my poor roommate through all of this emotional turmoil

My mom Penny for being my toughest critical read of the 1st draft

Elizabeth for being the blunt editor I needed

Janelle the design guru for great advice

Everyone who contributed to the Kickstarter to make this happen, because that was amazing

My friends at Principiadiscordia.com who influenced me creatively more than they think

The menagerie of friends who stick around somehow

and VNV Nation for the providing the soundtrack I needed to get through this. It's really incredible the power that music can have.

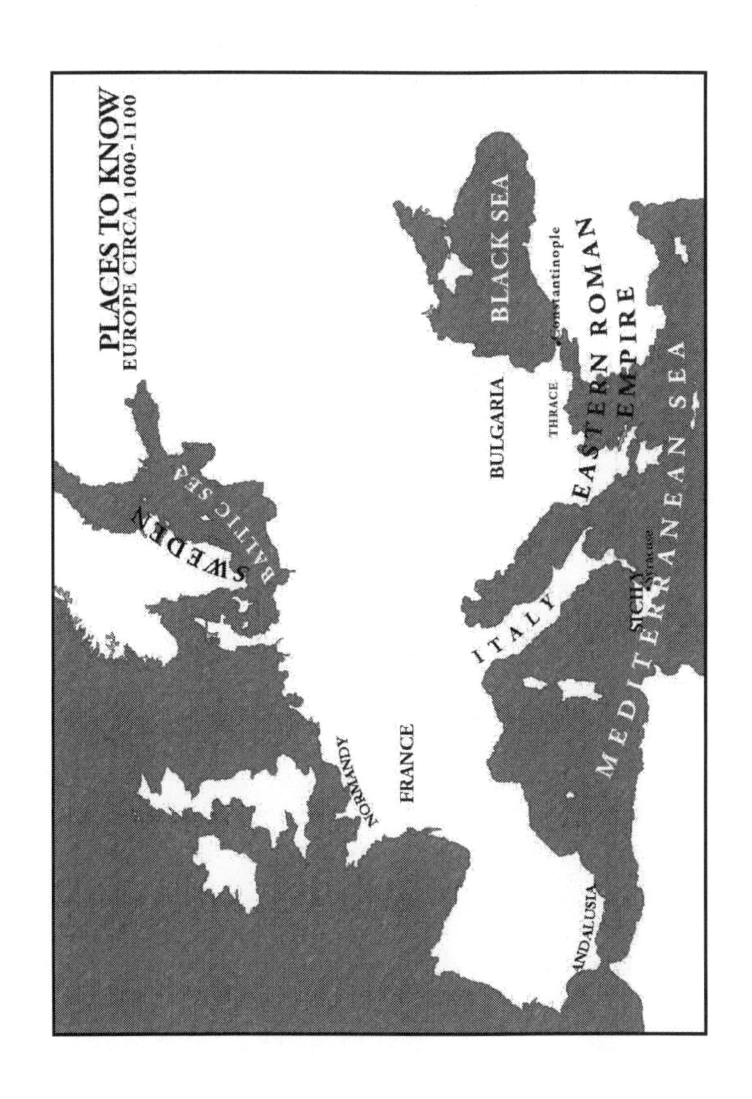
PLACES TO KNOW
EUROPE CIRCA 1000-1100
SWEDEN
BALTIC SEA
NORMANDY
FRANCE
ANDALUSIA
ITALY
SICILY
Syracuse
MEDITERRANEAN SEA
BULGARIA
THRACE
EASTERN ROMAN EMPIRE
Constantinople
BLACK SEA

INTRODUCTION

Constantine the Great became the sole ruler of the Roman Empire in the 4th Century. He moved the capital to a tiny Greek town called Byzantium, and there, he built his *Nova Roma Constantinopolitana*, the city of Constantinople.

Within a century following this event, the city of Rome would be sacked repeatedly by invading barbarian tribes until finally, in September of AD 476, the Germanic king Odoacer sent the Imperial Regalia from the Italian peninsula to Constantinople, effectively ending the twelve-hundred year rule of the Western Roman Empire.

The Greek speaking and Orthodox Christian Eastern Roman Empire, known in modern times as the Byzantine Empire, continued on the traditions for another millennium, and even referred to themselves as *Romanoi*, or Romans. Located at the passage in which the Silk Road entered Europe, the lifestyle of these people was a decadent one, and as the rest of the continent fell into the dark times of the early Middle Ages, Constantinople and the Empire thrived.

Beyond the mountains and along the boundaries of the northern reaches of land, another culture was beginning to be equally as influential on the shaping of medieval Europe: The Norse. Christianity had not come to these people yet, and their reputation among the settled lands of what is now England and France was not a good one. The Vikingr, men devoted to a lifestyle of trade, were known more for their aggressive raids on the coast and along the rivers than their expansion of commerce.

Scandinavians traveled deep within the eastern lands the continent, creating settlements in what is now Russia, and traveled down the great rivers to the Euxine Sea, where contact with the *Romanoi* were made.

Although conflict with them did occur, the Emperor Basil II, in the 10th century, sent out to make peace with these men, who called themselves *Varyags,* and hired them for assistance with rebellious forces out to take his throne. This started a tradition that would last through the Empire's last days; the tradition of the Varangian Guard.

Viking men from throughout Scandinavia would travel to the City of Gold for their chance at earning a fortune serving as the Emperor's personal bodyguards and the most elite fighting unit in the land they called *Greece.* They would be known and respected as the ax-wielding foreigners who swore a strong oath to protect and serve the Imperials of Rome...

PROLOGUE

The light of the sunset filtered through soft drapes of sheer silk into the halls of the Great Palace of Constantinople. Everything seemed quiet, eerily so, as the day was coming to a close.

In the corner of the complex, overlooking the gently lapping sea was a large imperial apartment which was building to become a scene of immense scandal.

There were moments of laughter and light conversation between a high ranking couple as their servant poured them their evening cup of wine as they returned from their meal with the Emperor. It happened so quickly, and the glass seemed to almost barely touch his lips. The man suddenly choked and struggled for air, unable to utter a single word in his pain, and his heavy metal tumbler of wine fell to the ground in a sickening clatter. He reached for his wife, who found herself helpless and frozen in panic as he collapsed in minutes of his first sip and agonizing until he finally found peace in death. The room had plunged into silence as the woman's cup was ripped from her hands by a guard and thrown across the room before she could follow.

The servant who had brought the wine dropped the bottle in her own horror, and ran toward the door, where she was stopped immediately by the guards. Without question, she was thrown to the ground and stabbed repeatedly, but the attention was drawn away from the scene of spilt blood, to one of an even greater loss.

"Stephanos?" the woman whispered into her husband's ear. "Please wake up."

Tears were filling her eyes as she gripped his limp hand where it hung at the side of the sofa where he had collapsed.

"Please...God..." She could barely see him beyond the tears and the purple veil of silk that was falling over her face from her gold and pearl hairpiece.

"No..." She shook her head, "No...No no no no no no..."

She gripped the fabric of his silk tunic on his shoulder, and attempted to shake him as she looked down into her husband's lifeless brown eyes.

She started to wail, and pray loudly as the room filled with servants, and family members who had heard of the poisoning of the favorite prince. She pressed her own face against his, smearing her cosmetics as her tears mingled with his last upon his lifeless cheeks.

"Anna…" A Varangian guard pulled her away from the body forcefully. "You need to get out of here." He said to her.

"No!" She fought, "No, Thorfinnr…I have to stay! Bring him back! Please! He can come back!"

"It doesn't work that way, child." The guard spoke in a heavy Norse accent as he turned the woman to face him, and cradled her head in his hands so that she could focus upon him as he spoke, "Look at me, Anna, look at me! There are no tears that can bring back the dead, but you will be soon to join him if you do not flee."

"THE EMPEROR HAS FALLEN ILL!" A voice cried from the halls of the palace, and another Varangian ran into the opened apartments, but stopped short at the sight of the bloodied servant, a dead man lying on his sofa, and the lady weeping loudly in the other guard's embrace.

"By the gods… It's a plot."

-One year later.

The spring thaw was coming to an end, and a farmer pulled his single horse along to his field to begin to plow the earth. He looked sadly to the ground, and pulled his woolen cap tighter over his ears to ward off the chill coming off of the nearby sea that still held the bite of the waning Baltic winter.

He lead his horse in silence to the edge of the field, and walked to its side so that he could mount the saddle, but before he could, a heavy bag of shining gold coinage was dropped at his feet. The farmer jumped back startled, and looked up at the grinning man who had dropped it.

"Is this enough of a reason for you?"

There was as stark contrast between the way the two dressed, the farmer was in layers of linen and wool with worn-out and stained embroidery, while the other was equally layered in silk and velvet, with richly embroidered stripes down his shoulders common in the fashions of the eastern lands.

The farmer shook his head, "And leave this?"

"Yes!" The other man laughed, "And leave this...Look at it! It's just dirt! What I have now is greater than any dirt or plant that grows from it. I have the respect and command of the guard of the Emperor! You were once a great warrior, and you went and made yourself a digger of holes in cold earth because of something that startled you in a dream. Dreams are just that, Ragnvaldr. They are nothing more than a shadow of a fear in your brain. Come: serve me!"

The farmer sighed, and knelt to retrieve some of the coins from the bag to get a closer look. They were freshly minted with the profile of the new Emperor, and shone like the sun even in the clouds of the north.

"Why did you even bother coming back, Thorfinnr?" the farmer asked, "I know it wasn't to pick my sorry ass up. Was it? You have passed through these lands many times on your journeys to the Empire and back. You have stayed at my home, eaten my grains and left within days, and yet now, you beg that I come with you this time."

"You've told me before that you wished to see the City of Gold, let me take you there. You will not be asked again, as this is to be my final contract. This is your chance!" The well-dressed man picked the bag up and snatched the gold from the farmer's awestruck gaze. Without allowing him so much a moment for thought, he simply grinned again and said: "Great, let's go!"

–

The sun was setting over the warm, glistening waters of the Mediterranean Sea. At the base of a steep incline, a woman was seated on a large rock on beach, and let the warm water wash up over the hem of her red linen dress. She sat in silence, and watched as the sun drifted closer and closer to the horizon of the sea to the west. Something caught her eye on the shore, and she stood up, allowing her bare feet to sink into the soft, wet sand.

Bending over, she retrieved a particularly spiny shell from a tidal pool and brushed the sand from it to get a closer look. The creature inside became frightened by the touch and retreated back into its shell, leaving a sticky residue on the woman's hand, which startled her, not realizing the snail was active. She dropped the shell on a rock, and it shattered, leaving the creature exposed. A nearby gull was quick to notice this, and swooped into retrieve the mollusk, leaving nothing but the shattered shell and traces of purple dye on the rock. The woman looked at her hand, and realized that the residue had also turned purple, and went to wash it off in the water.

"In our ancestors' time, that would have been a powerful omen." A man's voice came from above on a low cliff.

"It doesn't make it any less disgusting." She replied, checking her hand to see if it needed additional washing.

"Anna." He continued, "You have to go back."

The woman sighed and resigned to washing her hands in the seawater again, but he continued nonetheless.

"Do it for me, for our family, and everything that we stand for."

"I know." She replied softly, "I know..."

A few of the children from the city were not far off-shore, laughing as they were returning from their day swimming along the coast. The woman reflected on her day as a youth doing the same, and smiled to herself.

"Perhaps I will swim first."

The man's voice laughed, "Do you think you still can?"

"Does one ever truly forget?"

"Then it will be a sight indeed for the Saracen men in the port to see a woman in the water. Especially if you thrash about like you used to."

"Well, if I'm fortunate, perhaps one will write a song about it someday."

"You give the infidels too much credit."

"All men sing, father." She stood on the rock and squinted up toward the cliff where he stood, "Just of different sirens."

"There is no different siren than yourself, girl." The man reached a hand down toward his daughter, "But you cannot defy the Purple. Not without consequence."

CHAPTER 1
THE CITY OF GOLD

The gate opened to allow the small caravan of goods and travelers into the glistening city of Constantinople one early August morning. The streets, just beginning their daily routine of commerce, paused to watch the latest arrival of nobility to the palace of the Empire. Dignitaries often came and went, but the presentation of this particular entourage displayed the pageantry usually associated with that of the Imperial Family: slaves and servants carrying parcels and leading horses and mules with carriages full of more crates and packages surrounded a larger, more ornate enclosed carriage, the type whose cargo was typically human.

It was difficult to say who it was, but the lack of purple, aside from the insignia worn by the guards that accompanied the arriving party, proved it was no one born directly into the family, but someone of importance nonetheless.

The caravan snaked its way through the streets of the crowded city until it reached the Great Palace. The gates opened and swallowed it whole, leaving the commoners on the streets in wonderment as to who the latest visitor was.

The Emperor had died in the previous year, and the Empire found itself amidst turmoil as a controversial nephew took the throne. Relatives from the far reaches of the territories were expected to come and pay tribute to him, as well as his new empress. Although the visitors had slowed considerably, an entourage or two still came occasionally, even almost a year later. However, the circumstances of this arrival were different.

Horns sounded as the main carriage pulled to the entrance of one of the larger chambers with the Great Palace complex, and a heavily decorated Imperial guard exited to greet the party.

"My *Kyria*, we welcome you home to Constantinople," he said, as he reached a hand to assist a robed woman out of the larger carriage. "I trust your journey from the harbor was without incident?"

"Yes," she responded quietly, and raised her eyes to the structure of the Imperial palaces before her. Her silk shawl wafted in the breeze coming from Propontis, and danced in a fury of red and gold around her frame with her face devoid of any emotion as she gazed at the cold marble ahead of her.

"I understand that you must be weary from your voyage, *Kyria*, but the Emperor has requested your audience upon arrival. Porters will arrange to have your belongings brought and set up in your apartments." The guard put a hand on her arm. "I apologize for this inconvenience."

The lady nodded. "If it is what His Imperial Majesty demands, than we must comply." She made little eye contact with the guard as he led her indoors and into the massive, ornate hall where the court awaited her arrival. They stopped only once to allow her silk cloak to be removed by a servant, revealing the woman's face, surrounded by a veil of pearled silk and silver ornaments. Her body was draped with a wrap of even more embroidered silk that covered her linen dress, which was embellished with nothing more than the traditional *clavii* of the Imperial fashion.

Her eyes were tired and heavy, light blue was their color, which contrasted sharply with her dark hair and tanned skin, and they focused on the tiled floor, rather than the movement occurring around her.

A herald stepped before the lady and the guard then led them both into the hall. "Now announcing the arrival of Anna Dokeianina Syrakousina, the wife of Stephanos Komnenos: cousin to his Imperial Majesty."

The lady found herself pushed in front of the guard gently, and walked behind the herald hastily with her chin held high until she reached the dais where the Emperor of the Roman Empire sat in state beside his wife, and then knelt almost immediately on the ornate carpets and cushions placed in front of the thrones. Her eyes fell away from the monarchs and immediately to the floor, demonstrating her subservience to the Purple.

"*Kyria* Anna." The Emperor stood from his throne, stepped down from the dais, and reached a hand out for the woman to take. "Welcome to my court."

Anna took his hand, and kissed the large ring he wore that bore the Imperial insignia. "My Emperor," she said softly, still not looking up to make eye contact. "Thank you for your hospitality."

"My heart goes out to you, dear wife of my deceased cousin. His loss has surely been felt throughout the family, and we welcome you as one of our own."

"Your generosity is most thanked, My Emperor." Anna let go of his hand, and looked up only briefly as she placed her hand across her chest. At first she thought that the empress had remained seated, but in fact she was standing as well, but was considerably shorter than her husband. She was but a child, and the Emperor was at least forty years her senior. The thought sat uneasily with the lady, and she closed her eyes to hide disgust, and brought her gaze back to the floor.

"I hope that you find your days here in my capital comfortable, *Kyria* Anna," the Emperor intoned. "As your husband was my cousin, so shall you be my cousin, and as he was a prince of Rome, so you shall be from this day forth: a princess, bearing forth all the rights and privileges bestowed of the title. Your family in Sicily shall benefit from your late husband's pension, and you are free to live where you choose. Chambers have been arranged for you here in the palace, along the edge of Propontis so that it may remind you of your island home as a child. Please stand."

Anna obliged the Emperor's wishes and stood slowly with his aid. "Yes," he said, touching a hand to her cheek, "I feel that you will find your life here back in the Great Palace most pleasurable."

Anna disliked his touch, but dare not pull away, and looked to the left of the Emperor, where his guards stood, and her eyes met those of one of the guards briefly. She saw only a flash of deep blue from his gaze before he realized she was looking at him and turned away.

"Thank you, again, my Emperor, for your gracious hospitality and gifts in this time of mourning," she replied, and gave a deep bow to remove his touch from her face. "My husband's mysterious poisoning is a dark time for our family and Empire indeed, but I feel that I shall overcome this strongly."

"Good," the Emperor nodded. "Once you make yourself comfortable in your new home, you and I will discuss the option of a new marriage for you. A lady, if not princess of my court, of your age is still a valuable asset."

"I understand, my Emperor."

"You may have your leave to your chambers. My guard, Ioannes, who escorted you in, will show you around."

"Thank you, my Emperor." Anna gave another bow, and turned her back; slowly meeting the gaze of the guard before her, she walked toward him hastily.

The walk was in silence for the most part, until Ioannes said softly, once they turned a corner and made their way toward the Boukoleon Palace on the water, "He doesn't trust you."

"For the duration of my marriage, there were three separate Emperors, dear guard," Anna replied. "They trust no one."

"He is an especially dangerous man, *Kyria.* He was in exile for many years…" Ioannes trailed off as he noticed Anna's eyes wander out toward the other side of a courtyard where several of the Emperor's guards were standing. Eyes met yet again, and her pace slowed.

"*Varangoi,*" Anna said, pausing while she watched them for a moment, or more specifically he -- the one who had looked at her in the court, and who once again looked away. "The only men any Emperor could trust."

"Indeed," Ioannes replied. "Men of the north, hired for a price to protect the Purple, and only the Purple. Dangerous, if I do say so myself. I never found myself fond of mercenaries."

"There has never been a recorded breach of contract between the Varangians and their Emperor in the century of their existence," Anna stated. "They are there to protect the crown. I fear them not."

The guard with the blue eyes turned again to catch Anna's gaze, and this time held it for a bit longer. It felt like minutes had passed with them locked in a fixed stare, but it was merely seconds, and Ioannes took Anna's arm, which caused her to jump.

"Come," he said. "You need your rest, I'm sure."

Anna began to walk with her escort, and turned back to see the Varangian once more, and he continued to watch her until she turned the away from the courtyard.

"That woman," he spoke in his native tongue to one of his fellow guards. "She is not safe here. Princess or not."

"If you continue to look at her, the Emperor will have your eyes," the other guard replied.

"It is her eyes that intrigue me so," he with the blue eyes replied, and turned away from the corridor once Anna was out of sight.

"We are here for the Emperor. We do not question his motives. We are here for our pay, and when our contract is fulfilled, we can go home," his comrade said. "Do not find yourself attached to these weak and decorative peoples, Ragnvaldr. You can have any woman in Sweden when you return home with your fortune."

"I never said I wanted her. I was merely looking at her."

"What is this commotion?" Another, more senior member of the Varangians stepped out. He was taller, slightly older and more ornately dressed in rich velvets and silks, which demonstrated the many years of service needed to afford such fineries.

"Nothing, Thorfinnr," Ragnvaldr sneered.

"Your new man here thinks it's OK to stare at the Emperor's cousin."

Thorfinnr shrugged. "He can look, he just can't touch."

"Surely, touching can't be that bad." Ragnvaldr raised an eyebrow.

"Aha! So you were doing more than just looking then," the other guard stated. "I knew it. He's going to get us all in trouble, Thorfinnr. His behavior has already been a problem."

"I brought you down here so that you may find the glory you were speaking of back in the cold." Thorfinnr got in Ragnvaldr's face. "You complained of being bored, and wanting to find treasure. You were nothing more than a farmer in the bogs, and yet I offered you this opportunity of a lifetime: do NOT screw it up. You make me look bad, and you make all of us look bad. Ladies of the court, especially those in the Imperial Family are very much off-limits. There are whores in town for that."

Anna turned back again, even though now out of sight of the courtyard, she paused, despite the guard's insistence.

"I know that voice!" She said.

"I was only looking…" Ragnvaldr protested.

"…And she was looking back," the other guard interjected. "Curious, I'm sure, as to why a lowly guard would even pay her the time of day."

Ragnvaldr sighed and looked down. "I get it. No more looking."

"Thorfinnr?" Anna pulled completely away from Ioannes at this point, and began walking back toward the courtyard. "Thorfinnr, is that you?"

"Sounds like you're about to get a second glance, anyway." The other guard scoffed.

"I hear you!" Thorfinnr answered the calls in Greek, "Roman brat, yes it's me!"

Ragnvaldr looked away, and mumbled, "I need to go back to work." And walked off before Anna could reach the men.

She walked over with no ceremony, and the two remaining guards made no attempt at humility before one of their superiors.

"You came back!" She exclaimed and threw her arms around the silk-clad guard in surprise.

"I could ask the same about you…" He replied, holding her close, "Why are you here?"

"I had to…"

"Hey!" The other guard stood there and cross his arms, "What about me?"

"I know you would never leave, Tiernan." Anna smiled at the other guard and pulled herself from the embrace with one to be simply transferred to the other.

"Was there not another guard here earlier?" Anna asked after Tiernan received his proper greeting, "A new man, I have never seen him before."

"New recruits." Thorfinnr replied, "We have many new men this season. I shall be a busy, busy man keeping the lot in line."

"Are you not in my service, then?" Anna asked.

"I wasn't aware that you owned me exclusively, my *princess.*" Thorfinnr teased. "And no, I am not. For His Imperial Majesty has felt that I deserved a raise of pay. I am now Captain of the Guard."

Anna's face visibly showed disdain, and Tiernan laughed.

"I know. I take pity on the man as well."

"Are you alright, child?" Thorfinnr asked. "You look suddenly pale."

"Congratulations." She said softly, "It was well deserved after all these years of service to my family and his. I just suddenly feel less welcome, or safe."

Thorfinnr nodded, "I will see to it, on every inch of my blade, that you are protected and safe, and as much as it pleases me to see you alive and well, know that seeing you back in Constantinople after what happened makes me extremely uneasy as well. Keep your wits sharp, and your blades sharper, Anna. I fear that both of us were not summoned back for a banquet."

--

Weeks passed, and business was as usual in the capital. Anna was once again accustomed to life at the palace, so after the months she spent away after the death of her husband, adjusted back into the life of a princess in the Imperial Court. She sat there in state with the ladies to the right of the empress, wearing gold trimmed in purple to show her status as a lady of high rank, and her hair woven in a net of gold with pearls and shells of her homeland, as a similar strand around her neck did likewise display. She was never fond of court, and found herself daydreaming until pulled from it sharply by the Emperor's shrill voice.

Pilgrims were returning from the Holy Land through Constantinople. The roads were growing dangerous with the encroaching Seljuk Turks pressing into the Roman borders. Tensions were high with the onset of war, and rumors were being spread that these new infidels were torturing those striving to reach the Holy Sepulcher, and yet, still, travelers from the west continued to flow through Constantinople to attain their dream of walking in the footsteps of Christ at the Holiest of Holies.

This particular set was Norman, known for their disdain of the Empire. They had called for an audience with the court as the lord that commanded them was of high rank for a Latin, and was a confidant of the previous Emperor, but was unaware of his passing. This was creating a tense, difficult situation.

"I have no patience for this." The Emperor stood, frustrated with dealing with conversation in Latin and not Greek, as his knowledge of the language was failing him. Rubbing his eyes, he surveyed members of the court until he looked upon Anna.

"You."

Anna looked to her sides and said softly, "Me, my Emperor?"

"Yes, you. You were born in lands to the west. Surely you speak the language of the Pope better than that of the One True Church."

Tensions were high between the Latin Catholics and Orthodox Greeks since the official split just decades earlier, and the Emperor made his disdain unfortunately all too clear when dealing with these western pilgrims.

"I was raised by Romans and have spoken Greek my entire life…"

"But you are well educated in Latin as well. You had to have been, living near Rome."

"I feel that his Imperial Majesty should also be well-educated in the ways of the language of the Caesars," Anna muttered, but not softly enough and the Emperor's look upon her turned into that of a glare.

"I know the language of the Caesars, but more importantly I speak the language of Christ!" he shouted and it echoed throughout the hall. "Now, come here and do what I demand of you, and I will deal with your insubordinate words later."

Anna put her eyes down from the Emperor, but didn't lower her chin as she stood from her chair, and stepped gracefully toward the Latin visitors.

They were armored and dirty, and Anna reached for her perfumed handkerchief and brought it closer to her face to mask their odor, but maintained a calm disposition despite how she was just treated.

"*Salvete omnes*," she said softly, greeting them in Latin, and the obvious leader of the group, wearing the clothing style of the Normans, stepped forward and bowed.

"Resplendent lady, thank you for lending your voice to us so that his Imperial Majesty may hear us."

"The pleasure, I'm afraid, is not entirely all mine." Anna nodded, and the group smiled at her words. "What brings you to Constantinople, and why are you seeking the audience of the Emperor of Rome?"

"Ah, yes, my lady," the Norman spoke. "My men and I are returning from Jerusalem. We ask for nothing more than the hospitality of our Christian brothers here. We require room and board for no less than a week while we wait for our ship and continue our journey home to our freehold in Andalusia. Please share our condolences as well, for we were unaware that the previous Emperor had passed."

"I will tell my Emperor." Anna turned and swallowed, looking back in the direction of the Emperor and then down, once again, to his feet, and spoke to him, in Greek: "They await their ship home and ask for lodging and food, as they are fellow followers of Christ returning home from Jerusalem."

"They come into my palace like simple beggars asking for handouts?"

"They come in as great nobles of Andalusia and pilgrims of Christ, set out by your predecessor." Anna looked up and made eye contact. "You should grant them their request."

"Do NOT advise me again, *Prinkípissa* Anna! Sit down -- your work is done…no, wait…tell them I shall grant their request, for no longer than a month's time. Apartments shall be prepared in one of the palaces for their disposal, ONLY because of their relations with my predecessor."

"Yes, my Emperor." Anna turned back to the Norman and his men. "You may stay for no longer than a month. Chambers will be prepared."

"Thank you, my princess." He knelt this time, and his men followed. Once they stood, Imperial guardsmen came and escorted them out of the Great Hall, and Anna slowly returned to her seat, but the Emperor caught her arm before she could and dragged her out in front of the court.

"You dare speak out against me? In front of my

people? In front of those visitors?"

"You dare treat me as a servant or lowly translator?" Anna said, struggle in her voice before he let her go and she fell onto the steps on the dais.

"Foolish woman. Just as foolish as my cousin whom you married…" the Emperor sneered.

"You are also foolish to call upon a lady in the court to speak when you should know the language yourself." She rubbed the sore spot on her arm. "You should show strength and intelligence, not lethargy and ignorance, or, for that matter, arrogance."

"I should have you killed for your treachery!"

"I mean no treachery! Treachery is done to usurp the throne, and I don't have a death wish."

"Unlike your husband, you mean?"

With those words, Anna rose to her feet suddenly, but before she could move any further, two Varangians had her by her arms, and held her back as she struggled. The entirety of the court stopped to watch as a princess of the Empire was suddenly held captive by the Emperor, but yet, out of their own fear, they remained silent and useless.

"Hah! Indeed I hit a bit of a sour note." The Emperor moved toward her, and struck her in the face with an open palm. "For now on, you do as I command. You come when you are called; you will answer with nothing more than the word 'yes'. You are lucky that I will not kill you for your behavior." He lightly touched the red mark on her cheek. "No, I will make an example of you in other ways."

Stepping away from her, he spoke to the Varangians. "You." He pointed to one of them. "With the ax. You will stay with her at all times. She is to only leave her apartments if I summon her, or for meals, or for the liturgy. She is never to be out of your sight until I see fit to release her from house arrest."

Anna heard as one of the guards spoke to the other, obviously translating the Emperor's words into Norse so that he could understand better.

"Take her away, until I feel like looking at her again." The Emperor returned to his throne, and the guards took the princess out of the hall, and back toward her wing of the Boukoleon with no incident. She only looked up once to see which guards had her in custody, and, sure enough, it appeared that the blue-eyed one whom she had noticed on her arrival would indeed be the one assigned to her.

"*Kyrie Eleison*," she swore to herself, and looked back down until they reached her doors. Servants, surprised to see her in the keeping of the guards, quickly opened her chambers to allow them in.

Instead of throwing her as the Emperor did to make a show, they both let go of her gently, and the guard that was not assigned to her came forward and bowed to her. "I am sorry, my princess," he said, his northern accent heavy, before leaving her quarters, and Anna in silence with her jailer.

Anna put a good amount of distance between them

quickly, and he stood there, staring down at her.

"So," she said after several moments of total silence. "It looks like you and I will be spending a significant amount of time together, Barbarian."

She walked over to one of the large sea-facing windows and pulled back the drapes, allowing the natural light to illuminate the entire large drawing room. After more silence, she turned back to the guard, standing where he previously was, and still staring at her.

"You can speak to me; I will allow it," she said, pulling back more curtains, and then looking toward him again. "It's quite all right: you may be at ease with me."

There was still no answer.

"Oh, right. Do you not speak Greek?"

Nothing.

"*Latinum? Tu Latine loqui?*"

Again silence, and Anna showed her frustration. "Right. Of course not. Barbarians speak like 'bar bar bar'!" She laughed a bit, but stopped, knowing that the joke, although a classic since ancient times, was inappropriate in his company.

"He probably put you with me because you cannot speak to me. Naturally … leaving me in silence so that any words I speak out against him are lost," Anna sneered, and walked into her dressing chamber where a servant awaited her to help take down her hair.

The Varangian followed slowly and stood in the arch to the dressing room and watched as Anna's hair was uncrowned, unnetted and unbraided carefully by the Persian woman in her charge.

"My princess…the guardsman?" she asked, in a heavy Persian accent.

"I have been placed under house arrest for speaking out to the Emperor in court."

The servant sighed. "Anna, my princess, you have always been strong, but at times there is more strength in silence than words."

"I suppose I shall learn my lesson eventually," Anna smirked and looked up at the guard, who again, was fixated upon her, until their eyes met.

"How long will he be here for?"

"I don't care."

"What?"

"Huh?" Anna broke her gaze. "Oh, until the Emperor says so."

"Having one of those northern men in here makes me feel uneasy. He couldn't assign you a Greek guard?"

"I think I'm safer with the Varangian." Anna looked up at the guard again, but this time he was deliberately avoiding eye contact.

--

Three days passed. Anna was still unable to leave her room and eventually just requested that all meals be brought to her instead of having to leave and face the courtiers in a dining room. The silence between her and the guard was full of tension, but still, his presence to her felt more comforting than the cold marble floors of sitting in state.

On Sunday morning, Anna was sitting by a window in her parlor, wearing nothing more than a simple tunica, reading the Psalms to pass the time, when Ioannes opened the doors to her apartments.

The Varangian moved forward but then stood down when he saw the Imperial guard, and stepped aside to let him in.

Anna continued to sit, and looked up at Ioannes when he entered her parlor.

He looked away slightly, realizing she was under-dressed, but spoke anyway: "The Emperor calls upon you to attend the liturgy today. He expects to see you escorted to the Empress's loge of Hagia Sophia in one hour's time."

"Very well." Anna closed her Psalter and set it on the table in front of her. "Leave me to get dressed and I will … gladly … attend the liturgy."

Ioannes nodded, and continued to avert his gaze as he left the parlor past the Varangian, looking up only briefly to view him, as if he had disdain for the lower class foreign man being in a room with an underdressed woman.

In the short amount of time it took Anna's servants to dress her, she managed to gain about thirty extra pounds in pearls, silver, gold, and silk in her favorite reds and greens. Her hair was braided in what seemed like three times over and piled atop her head to support the gilded ornaments and falls of jewels that danced beside her face. She sighed heavily in the heat of the Mediterranean summer, and then motioned for the Varangian to open the door and lead the way to the basilica.

CHAPTER 2
BROKEN BARRIERS

Hagia Sophia was connected to the Great Palace by a special designated walkway just for the Imperials. Dozens of onlookers would often wait to see the Imperials process to their weekly worship, dressed in the full, decadent splendor of Byzantium. Anna was permitted to lead the way herself, but her Varangian jailer was close behind, as well as the usual gaggle of attendants that follow the court ladies onto the balcony in case any of them dropped something or needed something, and so they also could partake in their Orthodox rite.

The Varangians themselves were allowed to maintain the religion of their homeland, but were still required to attend church liturgies and functions in service to the Emperor and the Imperial family as a whole. As Anna took her seat in the loge to watch the proceedings below in the basilica, Ragnvaldr moved back a good distance to where he could still watch her, but not be driven to partake in the ceremonies. However, the traditional, heavily chanted Orthodox Liturgy takes hours, if not easily half the day, and it wasn't long before he became terribly bored.

He paced back and forth for at least forty-five minutes, and after that became old and he had grown tired of the beautiful songs being sung by the congregation in the basilica, he found himself counting stones in nearby mosaics. When that lost its allure, he pulled from his belt pouch a small file used to keep the nails trimmed, and picked at dirt beneath his fingernails before scratching into a marble wall to see if it would leave a mark. After a time, he looked over his shoulders several times to see if the ladies were still completely fixated on the liturgy; he began to carve furiously into the marble, inscribing it with a random saying in the runic alphabet of the Norse.

Anna had been engrossed in the proceedings for quite some time, but feeling her own boredom grow, decided to turn her head slightly to see where the Varangian was. Catching him out of the corner of her eye, during the singing of a particularly arduous chant, she quickly snapped her head around to stare at him, mouth slightly agape as he defaced the sacred church carelessly. Fortunately no one seemed to notice her head a-turn, so she remained fixated on Ragnvaldr until he acknowledged her stare, and froze in place, realizing he had been caught.

Anna raised an eyebrow, her shocked expression plainly saying: "What are you doing?!" and then shook her head slowly and lightly from side to side, signaling him to stop.

Ragnvaldr smirked a bit, and quickly put his file away.

Then, as if nothing had happened, he looked away from Anna and walked from the defaced wall, beginning to pace yet again.

Anna couldn't help it, and cracked a smile, laughing very softly to herself before returning her focus to the basilica.

--

Very few words were exchanged between the ladies of the court and Anna as they exited the basilica after the liturgy, and made their way back to the palaces. Ordered back to her chambers yet again, the Varangian made sure that Anna was back under her house arrest.

They arrived back in time for supper, and as they entered the foyer of her apartments, Anna began to remove the heavy ornaments from her hair without the aid of her attendant, who was having her meal in the kitchens with the rest of the servants. The area was quiet, and Anna began to undress herself without thinking twice. As she moved into her main chamber to place her elaborate headpiece down on a table and undo her braids, she sang a piece of the liturgy softly to herself.

"Does…your god answer you when you sing to him?" the Varangian asked suddenly as he followed and watched her.

Anna stumbled when he spoke and dropped a few strands of pearls on the floor at the sound of his voice. Her eyes snapped open at him, as she hastily leaned over to pick up her fallen jewelry.

"You!" she exclaimed. "You! You speak Greek!"

"Of course I do. I work here, do I not?" His accent was thick, and his words were slow, but this did not calm Anna's reaction.

"All this time … these last days I have sat in hours of silence, assuming you did not know the language, and you have been lying to me!"

"I did not know if I was permitted to speak with you."

"I asked you, and you did not reply! You have LIED to a member of the Imperial family, Barbarian, and for that I could have you executed!"

The Norseman remained calm. "Are you not in enough trouble with His Majesty? I doubt that he would believe you. That is, if you truly meant for my death."

Anna was silenced by his words, and just stood there in her own frustration for a few moments before speaking again.

"I do not mean for your death," she replied softly in the words of the Swedes.

The Varangian's blue eyes opened wide. "And you speak the language of my people!" he responded in the tongue himself.

"Some. I know the languages of the Northmen from their settlements on my homeland and what the Varangians have taught me in my youth. Which is why the Emperor called upon me to speak; but I spoke Latin so that I would not be insulted by the court for knowing the language of barbarians!"

"He means to insult you and your family because you are not Roman." The Varangian moved toward her.

Anna moved back as he came at her. "How dare you say such a thing? My family line in Syracuse goes back before Christ."

"Your eyes give you away."

"I tell no lies."

The Varangian was upon her then and backed her into a wall, taking her face in his hand. Anna immediately began to struggle, but he overpowered her greatly.

"Your eyes, they are blue as the ice of the East Sea, princess. Those are not the eyes of a true, pure-blooded Roman. They are the eyes of the Germans and other men of the North. Your skin may be tan and your hair dark, but your line is not as ancient as you say."

"Let me go!" Anna tried to move, but the guard held her tight. "Or I will have your head for this!"

"I mean you no harm, and I will not hurt you, princess -- just listen!" He held onto the sides of her face tightly, "Your eyes are blue as your mother was of the North, was she not? It is how you know the language!"

Anna closed her eyes and the Varangian let her go.

"Normandy," she said softly. "My mother's line is of Normandy … now let me go."

The Varangian smiled and loosened his hold on her. "Brothers are we, the Swedes and the Normans. More distant now than we used to be, but we still share words." He took a few steps back to allow the woman to regain her composure. "I knew. I knew from the first day you stepped into the court that you had blood of the North."

Anna remained against the wall, catching her breath and rubbing her face and shoulders where he had held her. "I was raised Roman, speaking Greek in a proper household of my father's before I was married and brought to Constantinople many years ago. I have not seen my mother since I was but a girl. She passed on nearly a decade ago." Her words returned to Greek, out of ease for herself, and to put the barbarian in his place.

"When was the last time you returned home?" he easily followed suit.

"After my husband died, I spent a year with my father and kin on Sicily. While I was away is when the Emperor was raised to the Purple. My return was when you saw me in court. I was summoned back, as my place is in the courts of Rome, as the island now belongs to the Saracens and the Normans."

The guard raised a brow: "And this is bad?"

"I may be half Norman, Varangian, but I was raised a Roman, in Roman cultures and of the Greek Liturgy, not the Latin. My place is here, now."

"You may call me by my name, instead of so plainly as your word, *Varangian*."

"You must tell me your name before I can use it."

"Ragnvaldr," he said. "Ragnvaldr Gunnarsson."

"Well, Ragnvaldr." She regained her posture. "I am Anna Dokeianina Syrakousina. Was that so hard?"

He laughed a bit. "Your name is very long."

"Well, it is my first name, my family name, my married name and where I am from. My name is Anna, my father's family is Dokeianos, I am from that part of the family once of Syracuse. It is how we name ourselves."

"I am only named for my father."

"What of where you are from? Are you of Kiev or Angleland? Or perhaps Norway like Thorfinnr?"

Ragnvaldr shook his head. "I am of Sweden. This is the farthest I have ever traveled from my home."

"Do you like it here in Constantinople?"

"Not terribly. No." He shook his head. "It is very different from my home. I did not want to come here."

Anna raised a brow and started to move away from the wall. "Then why have you come here?"

Ragnvaldr sighed. "Thorfinnr, the captain of the Varangian guard here, had returned from his contract wearing the finest silks and velvets, and bore with him many treasures that he was paid after the last Emperor died. I was but a simple farmer and had no desire to travel, but Thorfinnr came and promised the men a new life -- a life of wealth and prestige in the service of the Empire.

"'Come with me, Ragnvaldr,' he said. 'Come with me and see the City of Gold you have heard of in the east. I will show you glory and treasures.'

"So I did, and I followed him here to Constantinople and trained to be a guard. Here I have been now for half the year."

"I have known Thorfinnr for many years. He is a good man and served my family and the former Emperor well." Anna moved toward a table where her meal had been spread out for her. "Will you join me for supper?"

"I am not permitted to sit with the Imperials for meals." He bowed and backed away.

"You eat what I cannot after my fill, anyway, Ragnvaldr. Please, sit with me. Who is here to say otherwise? You?"

"If my lady demands it, then I shall." He took a nearby chair and waited for Anna to sit before he did.

There were a few moments of silence while Anna placed food on her plate and poured her wine, and noticed that Ragnvaldr did nothing.

"Please," she said, "eat. Please take your portion." She removed bread from a platter it was on and handed it to him, so that he would have his own plate. Then emptied a small bowl of fruit and filled it with wine for him. "Drink. There are no formalities in my private company."

Ragnvaldr nodded silently and took the wine. "The others, they told me about you. You are very different than the rest of them. You have your mother's northern hospitality."

"A woman's place is to ensure that no man at her table goes hungry, be him rich or poor," Anna replied, between bites of the bread in her hand. "I was raised to believe that every soul should live in comfort. You bleed red; I do not bleed purple."

"But a princess's place is not sharing a table with her guard," Ragnvaldr objected.

"I am not a princess of the blood. I am just a lady simply born to privilege and married to the Purple. Yet, would you deny a princess or any lady offering you a hot meal?"

"I suppose not." Ragnvaldr sipped his wine. "And I am sorry: I should not have touched you as I did."

Anna nodded. "No, you should not have."

"But I stood down. I will always stand down. I will never hurt you."

"I know."

"No, Princess, please, listen." Ragnvaldr leaned forward slightly so that he could lower his voice, as if he feared for anyone to overhear. "I will always stand down. The Emperor will not. You have but to ask me, and I will obey. Not only will his Majesty not obey your cries, but also I will have to watch and do nothing. Do not trust him."

Anna looked up as Ragnvaldr spoke, and the look on her face showed that she understood, perhaps too well.

"My Princess, you are safer here with me at your table, than you are with him in an open court."

A few more days passed, and the princess was released from her house arrest as long as the Varangian stayed by her side, especially since she was expecting important company.

"So you have a son, then?" Ragnvaldr asked, walking slowly beside Anna through one of the massive garden courtyards.

"Yes. He will be sixteen this year," Anna nodded, and looked away and distant for a moment. "He is practically a man now."

"Why is he not already here with you?"

"Well, he went away to school four years ago. I have seen him barely since. Not even when his father died was he able to take leave."

"You seem young to have a son that age, my Princess," Ragnvaldr said softly, watching out for others that could be passing through and disagree with him speaking to an Imperial.

Anna smiled. "I am twenty-nine. I was married when I was twelve."

"Then your beauty is truly exceptional," was the Northman's reply.

Anna couldn't respond, or, rather, didn't know how to respond to the compliment, as he was a subordinate to her; so instead she simply looked away and blushed, deeply.

"Mother!" was heard from across the courtyard, and Anna snapped out of it and rushed forward toward her son.

"Alexander!" she exclaimed and tearfully met her only child with open arms. "Look at you … you've grown into a man now! *Kyrie...Kyrie…*"

He was taller than his mother by nearly a head, and had the form of a lanky young man under a slightly oversized indigo- and red-embroidered tunic. The boy laughed at his mother's words and kissed her cheeks several times.

"It has been painfully too long, my mother. I cannot thank you enough for your letters through the years. I have missed you and father terribly."

Ragnvaldr looked on, his face blank, unsure of what emotion to show, if any, during this reunion.

Alexander noticed the Varangian and stood taller in an almost protective, if not competitive, manner. "So, mother, I hear your words have once again gotten you in trouble."

"Nonsense. His majesty simply does not have a sense

of humor." Anna smiled and looked over at Ragnvaldr. "This barbarian has been a fine companion this past half week."

Ragnvaldr winced at the word "barbarian", but said nothing, not with the young prince present.

"Very well. You always were good at making friends with foreigners," Alexander smiled at his mother. "Always the talker."

"Stories of other lands fascinate me, young Alex, as they should you as well. Becoming an ambassador to the Bulgarians, my son!" Anna reached up and played with her son's curly brown hair.

They started walking toward the main court hall, and Alexander scoffed.

"At the expense of my freedom."

"Now now, son," Anna rebuked him gently. "Marriage is a necessity. You are a prince of the blood; a *porphyrogénnētos,* no, but still as a member of the family you are needed to solidify important agreements between peoples."

"Much like you and father, then?"

"Yes," Anna nodded. "I was brought to Constantinople to marry your father to regain territory on Sicily..."

"Which didn't work." Her son interrupted.

"…Which didn't work. You will marry this Bulgarian

princess to maintain the peace of our borders." She stopped walking and took her son's face in her hands. "And I expect you to make me, as well as your father -- rest his soul -- proud."

Alexander nodded. "Yes, mother, even if it doesn't work. Though would it be dishonorable to call upon your wisdom once I am in my place among the Bulgars?"

"You will write to me as often as you see fit, and I will respond in kind." She leaned up and kissed him gently. "Now, to face the Emperor."

Anna remained silent for the most part while the Emperor spoke to her son about his duties abroad, and the marriage contract was brought out. Although the Bulgarian princess who was to wed Alexander was not present, her father was, and Anna witnessed him sign his daughter and her holdings over to her son as the head of his estate in the absence of his father. The ceremony would take place in Bulgaria when Alexander would arrive there at the end of the week. In addition to lands along the border that were gained for the Empire, a lasting peace was signed for, and Anna received a percentage of the bride's dowry, which was a significant collection of wealth.

A feast followed, and lasted for several hours, during which Anna was beckoned by the Emperor and introduced to a duke from France, who was a relative of the empress. He was a wealthy, but not terribly attractive, gentleman a few years younger than her, and visiting from his court to see the empress. Ragnvaldr looked on from where he was stationed guarding one of the doors, and felt a slight twinge as Anna was forced to sit next to this foreign man, dine with him, and converse with him. She seemed to share moments of uncomfortable laughter with this stranger, but even still, the smiles said enough. He didn't understand a lot of the customs of the Empire, but what he did realize was this was evidently all done for a probable marriage arrangement.

"So, my princess," The French man had an unusual accent in the Latin he spoke to her, "We have heard that there are issues here on your border. Turkish peoples coming in and causing problems, and that the Emperor has written a letter to our Pope."

This caught Anna off guard, "Did he now?"

"Rumors, I am sure." The duke smirked a bit, "Why would the great Roman Empire call upon the Latin Church for aid? Silly to think, don't you agree?"

"Well, I'm sure you are misinformed." Anna replied, "Because I couldn't possibly fathom the honest man you call Pope, who so righteously excommunicated the entire congregation of Hagia Sophia out of nothing more than spite to answer the cries of help from the very people he deliberately severed from his precious Latin church."

The duke's smirk faded, and he stood up from his chair without a word, and walked away.

As night befell the capital during the feast and the festivities began to break up late, Ragnvaldr escorted Anna back to her chamber.

"It must be difficult to sign your son's life away," he said softly.

"We do what is necessary. For the Empire," Anna replied. "Difficult, yes, but I also understand. He is a good man, like his father was, and he will do us all proud."

"What of that man you spoke with?" Ragnvaldr's question was forward. "Who was that?"

"A potential suitor," Anna replied. "A nobleman of France."

"Are you to marry him, then?"

"Would it upset you if I did?" She stopped and turned, and asked as if his answer would actually have any bearing on her fate.

Ragnvaldr was stumped by her words. The wrong answer could endanger his life, or, worse, hers.

"No," he said, hesitantly.

Anna smiled. "You are a good man, Varangian, but I feel that I have taken enough of your time here. Your service should not have been marked by the imprisonment of a defiant princess. Men like you deserve more prestige, and battle."

"I serve where I am told to serve," he replied. "Nothing more."

"Again, a loyal and true man." Anna got to the doors of her apartment, which were opened by night watchmen. "The women in your land must be thankful for your virtues."

"If the women of the North were worth our virtues, I assure you, Princess, my kin and I would not be here."

"Are they that vile?"

"We often joke that us men started going Viking in the spring to escape our wives."

"Do you have a wife that you are escaping, then?" Anna asked jokingly.

Ragnvaldr's response was solemn: "My princess needs her rest." He pointed toward her bedroom.

"Right," she replied, looking over her shoulder toward the archway leading the way. "I shall…"

The Varangian guard was already across the foyer, heading toward the servant's quarters of the apartment. "Sleep well," he said, with his back turned toward her.

Anna, confused, watched him walk off, but then made her way to bed.

--

The night was cool and still. The soft lapping of the moonlit Propontis outside of the windows was the only sound heard throughout the palace.

A shadow crept along the outer façade, and slid quietly through the open, silk-curtained window of Anna's foyer. Moving stealthily, it found its way into her darkened, unguarded bedchamber, where she lay by herself in a large, extravagant bed.

The shadow removed a black hood from his face, and pulled a thin long dagger from within the cloak. Anna stirred a bit in her sleep, and the assassin froze in place, but doing so failed to remain inconspicuous, and he knocked an ornament from the wall, which fell with a crash.

Anna sat up in her bed with a start, and immediately began to scream when she saw the figure in her room. Unarmed and naked beneath her covers, she was trapped, and her screams did little to deter the assassin from coming at her.

"RAGNVALDR! RAGNVALDR! HELP!" she continued to scream, and prayed that he would hear her. Sliding from her bed and grabbing a sheet to cover her body, she ran to the corner of her room, and started throwing heavy marble and glass vases and vials in the direction of her killer.

One did manage to hit him in the head, but it didn't do much to bring him down, instead, the assassin moved faster, and was upon the princess with haste.

"Feisty little one," he hissed at her, and brought the knife to her throat, but before he could strike, Ragnvaldr came up behind him and pulled him from the woman.

Anna sank to the floor as Ragnvaldr dragged the assassin into the foyer and struck him to the ground. The Persian servant quickly rushed to Anna's side and helped her gather the bed sheet around her more tightly, but

Anna crawled out of her room just in time to see Ragnvaldr take his axe down on the neck of the assassin; Anna screamed again, as she was splattered by a few droplets of blood scattering from the severed head.

It was then that the night watchmen finally entered the chamber with their long pikes, but looked confused as to what had happened. Hearing the cries himself from his patrol in the hall, Thorfinnr ran in behind them, saw Ragnvaldr with the decapitated assassin, and then ran to Anna's side.

"My lady, are you hurt?" he asked, and when she didn't respond immediately, turned her face to look at him, and held it still to force her to look at him. "It's me -- it's Thorfinnr. You know me, and you're safe."

Standing back up, he rushed out of the chamber to another Varangian he was patrolling with. "Awaken the Emperor! A member of the household has been under attack!" He yelled his command in Norse, and the guardsman ran off at once. Ragnvaldr remained standing over the body with his bloodied ax, catching his breath and glanced over at Anna, who had come out of her shock into a flood of tears, and was being held tightly by her servant.

A few moments later, the partially clothed Emperor stormed into the chamber. "What is the meaning of this?" he shouted, and then looked down at the lifeless head staring back up at him from a pool of dark, fresh blood.

"By the Lord! What happened?!"

"Princess Anna was attacked by an assassin as she slept," Thorfinnr spoke. "Ragnvaldr took him down."

"Where is she?" the Emperor asked, sternly.

"Here," Anna replied, standing slowly, wearing nothing more than the blanket still wrapped around her body, with spots of blood on her face and arms where they had landed.

"Are you all right, child?"

"I owe my life to this man," she said softly, looking at Ragnvaldr, who looked directly back at her and didn't break his gaze as he had previously. "Without this Varangian guarding me, I would be dead."

The Emperor stared at the two looking at each other, and growled, "Lucky for you, that he was able to come to your aid." He added, half sneering, "Otherwise, we would have lost you, my dear Dokeianina."

Thorfinnr listened carefully to the tone of the Emperor's words, and his eyes narrowed, feeling that something was off.

"Guards, remove this body and have someone clean up this mess!" the Emperor ordered. "I bet it was some Bulgar, trying to get at the mother of our new ambassador, indeed. Terrible people that they are. We will investigate this fully. No attack on a member of the Imperial Family goes unchallenged!"

"Come, my lady, let's clean you up…" The servant guided Anna away from the bloodied scene; Anna's eyes stayed on Ragnvaldr, but he looked away as soon as she was taken from his immediate sight. His eyes fell to the floor, as he watched drops of blood still coming off of his ax, forming a puddle below.

"Tread softly, Barbarian," the Emperor chided. "For next time, you may not be as fortunate."

"There will not be a next time," Ragnvaldr replied in Greek, which startled the Emperor.

"Of course not." The Emperor turned to leave. "Of course not … Indeed."

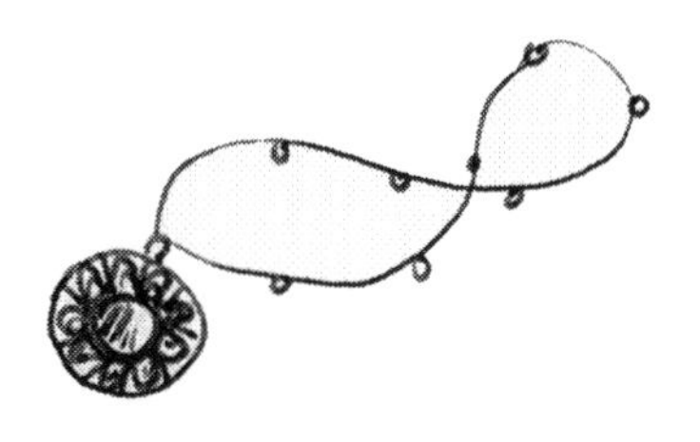

CHAPTER 3
BROKEN RULES

Two days had passed, and Anna was found sitting in the sunlit corner of the large courtyard nearest to her apartment. The sun warmed her skin through her layers of silk like she hoped it would, but it didn't brighten the color on her sallow cheeks and darkened eyes.

"You haven't slept," Ioannes said to her as he passed through the gardens.

"No," she replied softly, squinting from the reflection of light from the guard's armor.

Ragnvaldr was standing in the shade behind her, silent as he listened to the words of the Greek guard and the princess.

"The Emperor said that they have determined that the assassin was sent by the Bulgars."

"The assassin was sent by the Emperor." Anna looked up at the guard with exhausted eyes.

"Those words are treason, my princess." Ioannes looked from side to side, wondering if anyone else had heard her.

"I don't see you rushing to turn me in."

Ioannes sighed, and looked up at Ragnvaldr. "Keep an eye on her. As I have been told not to." He flipped a gold coin toward the Varangian and it landed at his feet. "For your service," he said hastily, before walking away.

Ragnvaldr reached down and picked up the coin. After checking its authenticity, he put it into a pouch on his belt nonchalantly. Getting paid extra for what he was already doing seemed like a good method to money-making.

"I fear for my life." Anna turned slightly so Ragnvaldr would hear her.

"As you should," he replied.

"I need to get out of the capital," she said, standing slowly.

"And go where?" Ragnvaldr asked.

"France, I suppose. I'll take that marriage."

"I would not think that it is wise. The Emperor is behind that set-up."

Anna paused thoughtfully. "They would strike Sicily first if I simply disappear, and my father would be killed for my stupidity."

"Or worse, your son." Ragnvaldr stepped forward.

"Or worse, my son." She nodded and her eyes fell to ground. "I never thanked you, properly, for saving my life."

"I was doing no more than my job, Princess," Ragnvaldr responded. "Nothing more than my duties already entail."

"Yet I feel my debt to you will never be paid," Anna said, and approached him. Reaching around her neck, she removed a long, gold chain with intervals of perfect saltwater pearls. As she retrieved the charm from within her dalmatica and handed it to him, Ragnvaldr's eyes lit up.

Instead of the typical cross or Christian icon that the Imperials dripped with, this was a unique round piece of hammered gold engraved with intricate knot patterns. In the center of the pendant was a large greenish cabochon of amber set in silver.

Ragnvaldr immediately reached for the pendant and began to examine it. "Where did you get this from?"

"It was my mother's, though as a child, she told me it was much older, and she remembered her grandmother wearing it as a brooch on her dress."

"I cannot take this, Princess," he said softly. "This is meaningful to you."

"So is my life," she whispered, and lifted the chain to place it over his neck.

Ragnvaldr bowed to accept it, and after Anna lowered the necklace onto his chest, she leaned up and gently kissed him on the cheek.

"Thank you," she whispered again, and slowly pulled back from him to head down the hall.

The Varangian took her hand as she stepped away, and she turned back to face him. Their eyes met as they had prior, only now, her hand was in his. They stayed like this for a moment until a voice broke the silence.

"*Princeps mea!*" It was the visiting Norman lord. "My princess!"

Ragnvaldr dropped her hand, and Anna felt her face burn at this sudden interruption.

"My lord," she smiled. "A pleasure to see you, as always."

"Indeed, yes." The lord glanced toward Ragnvaldr, who looked away; he could not understand their Latin conversation. "I heard of the assassin, and I pray that you are unharmed."

"Thank you," Anna nodded. "If it wasn't for this Varangian, I would most certainly be dead."

"As I have heard it as well," the Norman lord smiled. "Just as I am sure that I bore witness to what I was assuming you paying him your gratitude just now."

Anna felt her face grow hot again, and the lord smiled.

Ragnvaldr looked confused by the Latin conversation.

Anna replied in Norman, nearly whispering, "I speak

your language."

The lord seemed startled by this. "Apparently." He laughed a bit. "From the Varangian I would expect it, but certainly not a lady of the Greeks. It is not often that Norman anything is accepted. I'm surprised we didn't have to sleep outside of the walls."

"Her mother was Norman." Ragnvaldr entered the conversation now that he could. "This is why we she was asked to speak to you in court. Not for Latin. The Emperor meant to insult her."

"Insult her for speaking a language of the north." The lord shook his head. "I would call that having an important asset, and not anything to be ashamed of.

Anna nodded a bit and looked around; the courtyard was silent, almost too silent.

"I feel as if we are being watched," she whispered.

"Oh, no doubt," the lord replied, and then leaned in and spoke quietly. "But mark my words: your actions, and your affections, my children, are safe with me." He stepped back and cleared his throat: "So." His words returned to Latin as an Imperial Guard passed through. "I was sent here to see if you would care to join me at the Hippodrome as a guest of his Imperial Majesty for this afternoon's races."

"Ah." Anna followed suit, and Ragnvaldr stood at attention. "I would be honored."

The Hippodrome of Constantinople was one of the largest of its kind, and despite its age, was still very much in use centuries after it was built. It was home to an astonishing amount of Imperial history, and even though chariots were long out of fashion for regular racing, horse racing, various games and other ceremonies took place in the ancient structure still.

The three were able to enter the Imperial box, the *Kathisma*, through a path directly from the palaces, and the balcony opened to a view of a roaring, full crowd, the banners and pageantry associated with the customary games.

"Ah, Anna." The Emperor stood. "It is so wonderful to see you out and about after that dreadful night! Come, sit next to me, and bring our guest with you."

Anna grimaced at the idea of having to sit next to the Emperor, but complied with his orders, and the Norman lord sat beside her.

"So the princess is called Anna," the Norman said, in Latin. "What would she prefer I call her?"

"You may call me Anna. I am a princess by marriage only. What, sir, may I call you, then?"

"I am known as Patricius in the Latin language."

"Very well, then, Patricius." Anna smiled at the older gentleman.

"What are you two chattering about over there?" The Emperor butted in. "The games, they are about to begin!"

As the racers took their places at the starting line, flags of blue and green came to life in the seats of the common people. The ancient factions of chariot racing were now only ceremonial in nature, with their power over the government long gone.

"Chariots!" Patricius exclaimed. "Just as the great Roman Emperors of old held in Rome! How remarkable!"

As the races began, and the crowd became even more alive, the Emperor leaned over to Anna, and pointed at Patricius. "You should tell him a great tale of the circuses of Constantinople!"

Anna did not make eye contact. "And what tale would that be, my Emperor?"

"Ah, yes. Well, tell him of what the great Emperor Justinian did five centuries ago in this very arena!"

Anna fell silent.

"Tell him! Tell him of our great imperial power."

Swallowing, Anna leaned over to Patricius, and softly said, in Latin, "He wishes me of me to tell you of the Nika Riots."

Patricius looked over at her. "Riots?"

She nodded. "The Nika Riots were deadly. They say … tens of thousands were killed. The associations, the Blues and the Greens, collectively, were angry at the Emperor Justinian's new taxes, and his inability to pardon men for a murder that happened after a race. Two men escaped from their hangings and found sanctuary in a nearby church, which was soon surrounded by an angry mass of people. Justinian changed their sentences to imprisonment rather than death, but that was not enough. Another race was to be held a few days later, and the crowd came in tense and angry. Factions came together against the Emperor, and they began to chant *'Nika! Nika!'* which is Greek for, *'victoria'*, victory, and then stormed the palace. A dangerous and bloody riot broke out here, in the Hippodrome, and all over the capital, for a week. Fires destroyed over half of the city, including the Hagia Sophia and portions of the palace.

"The Emperor Justinian hid in his palace and it was the Great Augusta Theodora that told him to face his people and not flee in weakness. She is written to have said to him, 'purple makes a fine shroud.'"

"What have you said so far?" the Emperor interrupted.

"Just to the part of Theodora telling Justinian to face his people," Anna replied, turning back.

"Now, now, tell him what the great Emperor did!"

Sighing, Anna turned back to Patricius. "The people choose a new Emperor from the Green faction, and he was being crowned here in this very circus. Justinian, who remained hiding in the palace, sent a eunuch by the name of Narsus into the Hippodrome to face the mob unarmed and alone. He went straight to the Blues, holding a bag of gold. That eunuch told them that the new Emperor that they wished to have was a Green, and that Justinian always supported the Blues. The gold was distributed, and then the Blues stormed out during the coronation. This left the Greens stunned and alone in the circus, which were then slaughtered by imperial soldiers led by the great generals Belisarius and Mundus, and the riots soon after ended. Justinian had the new Emperor killed, exiled politicians that were against him, and rebuilt the city as he saw fit as he regained even more control."

"The Imperial Family has always been supporters of the Blues!" The Emperor took a blue colored flag out of his heavily ornamented cloak. "But Anna's family, going back generations, has always been supporters of the Greens!"

"Ancient traditions," Anna muttered. "The factions have not mattered for centuries! Even still, other great Emperors have been Greens as well!"

"I'm sure if you dare reveal it, you have a green flag on your person!" the Emperor scoffed. "Nero was a Green, you know, and he allowed Rome to burn to the ground!"

"Rest assured, my Emperor," Anna retorted, "if I dare reveal anything to you, it will be far less than a flag."

The Emperor raised his hand to strike Anna. "Why you insubordinate little ..."

However, she was taken by her hand and pulled to her feet as the games started and rushed to the front of the balcony by the Norman lord.

"He is going to kill you if you do not hold your tongue, Princess."

"He means to kill me anyway, no matter how I keep my silence." She pointed toward a particularly skilled charioteer -- one driving, surprisingly, for the Greens. "Him! Oh him! Watch! He's remarkable!"

Ragnvaldr's heart nearly leapt into his throat as he saw the Emperor raise his hand, but he closed his eyes and grasped at his long ax.

"I can end this," he thought, "in one swift move ..." Then he remembered his oath, and his payment, and the reason why he was in Constantinople serving as a Varangian guardsman to begin with.

Then his eyes went to Anna; his reason was changing.

"No." He shook his head as he continued to think. "No." But the images remained. He could bring her back to Sweden. He would wrap her in the finest furs and keep a large hearth during the winter to warm her, and she would be safe. Safe from … the only life she ever knew, the life of a high-ranking lady in the richest courts of the world. He looked at her. Anna's headdress dripped with strands of perfect pearls. Her ears were pierced with earrings of pure gold, silver and beautiful stones of green. Her dress was composed of layers of the finest linens and silks of the Empire, embroidered and beaded by a hundred hands in the Imperial workshops. Her skin was olive and naturally darkened by the warm Mediterranean sun that also kissed her dark hair with lightened streaks of gold. Her eyes were painted with the glitter of powdered gemstones and black kohl while her lips seemed constantly stained with the color of wine.

Anna was the glowing summer, where Ragnvaldr was the dark winter. She was the South, and he was the North. She was rich and soft, and he was poor and rugged from his work as a farmer in the bogs, here only, in her presence, by the very grace of the gods. What could be a gift from Freya was nothing more than a tease from Loki. He could not have her, and he would be forced to watch her die.

Anna continued to cheer on the charioteer with great excitement, which seemed to only anger the Emperor further. He rounded the corner of the first lap and the crowd became louder as a rider for the Reds attempted to get out of the way, but failed to control his horses evenly, forcing one to pull to the right away from the others, thus dragging the chariot off center, making it tilt and then tumble entirely, sending the rider into the wall.

"Oh, him!" the Emperor huffed as the Green charioteer passed. "He always costs me money in the bets."

Anna paid him no mind and watched with glittering eyes as he completed the race, and cheered with the rest of his Green fans as he crossed the finish line to the roar of the Roman crowd.

"I told you he was remarkable!" she exclaimed to Patricius.

The Emperor threw his blue flag to the floor, "Bah!"

Thorfinnr, who was standing behind the Emperor, took a few steps closer to Ragnvaldr.

"It appears your love has a bit of an admiration for that driver."

"Piss off, *rasshol.*"

Thorfinnr laughed a bit. "You can't keep your eyes off of her anymore."

"I mean to save her." Ragnvaldr no longer denied his affection. "I will bring her to the North, and she will be safe there with me."

"Ragnvaldr," Thorfinnr sighed, "these women … they are like flowers. They live for the eternal sun and warmth. Their golden robes are their petals and winter will cause them to wither. Let go of your attachment. She does not feel for you. See her as she cheers for a Greek? And keeps only the company of other nobles? She must love only her equals, and make only more decorative children that our children will be hired to serve. Also, she is old and worn. When you return home, you will have the money to find a young, virginal, new bride."

"I don't want a new bride," Ragnvaldr snarled.

"What are you two barbarians going on about?!" The Emperor turned and looked back at them. "You sound like … growling wolves when you speak. Utterly disgusting."

Thorfinnr took steps back. "Let it go. Just … let it go."

The crowd jumped to their feet when a fight broke out below in the arena over the results of the first race. Anna's hands went to her face.

"No!" she screamed.

The winner from the Green team was suddenly surrounded by a group of Blue charioteers who began to push and shove him forcefully. The man, plainly dressed in a yellow tunic, tried to avoid the blows and walk away, but they continued at him. Eventually, one of the Blues drew a sword, which he would learn would be a costly mistake.

The Green charioteer drew his own blade and was fast to block as a chop came at him, and, before anyone knew it, he was singlehandedly fighting off the opposition, four versus one, in what seemed to be an effortless dance of swordplay.

The Emperor stood to watch the spectacle, and even the Varangians and servants moved forward. Within seconds, one of the Blues lay dead, and the Green simply spun his sword in his hand, looking for more.

"By the gods!" Thorfinnr said, and Ragnvaldr just stood there in agreement with him. "Berserker!"

"Who is this man?" Patricius asked Anna, who just shook her head.

"I … really don't know," she replied. "I just watch him in the races!"

After the second Blue attacker fell, the Emperor shouted, "END THIS NONSENSE!" And the crowd suddenly came to a standstill. "Arrest those men! And bring that one, the Green, here!"

The Imperial balcony erupted with the thought of a common prisoner being brought up to the *Kathisma*, but nonetheless he was taken by guards and pulled along and upwards toward the Emperor and his court. Ragnvaldr put a hand on Anna's shoulder to escort her back to her seat, and she complied. The Emperor noticed this gesture, but said nothing, as he was more focused on the arrival of the prisoner.

He was tall, well-groomed, and wearing nothing more than a saffron-dyed tunic and worn sandals. He gave the guards little struggle as he was forced to bow in front of the ruling class.

"Who are you?" The Emperor stood and attempted to look ominous. "Where are you from? And why do you find it necessary to disturb my games?!"

"My name is Barabbas," the man replied. "I am from Cilicia, and ..."

"An Armenian!" the Emperor huffed. "I should have known only a rebel would have behaved this way."

Patricius leaned forward and examined the man. "Where did you learn to fight like that?" he asked, in Latin.

Anna went to translate, but Barabbas responded, "I have fought for many years with the people of my country, and served this Empire as well. I now make my living in the games, as I lost my home to the Turks, and my pension was cancelled due to my heritage."

"Anna!" the Emperor yelled. "What did they say?!"

"The Norman lord asked him where he learned to fight and this man stated that he once served in your armies, but his pension was canceled due to the fact he is Armenian and the Turkish invaders taking his land and making him flee. So he makes his living in the games."

The Emperor snarled, "One less mouth to feed, then." He sat back down. "Take him to the prisons. I will determine his bail when I see fit."

"On what charge?" Anna asked.

"On murder and disrupting my games. Much have you had already, Anna. Either you are quiet now or I will send you to share a cell with him!"

As Barabbas was taken away, Anna sat back in her chair in silence but looked over to Ragnvaldr briefly. He shook his head at her, and then looked away.

Patricius then looked at Anna. "How much is bail?"

"I dare not ask him now."

"I will take the prisoner to Andalusia with me. With skills like that he will be very well received among my men."

"He will probably make the bail unattainable for you on purpose," Anna whispered. "If you need assistance, I will give you additional funds to release him."

"My princess." Patricius bowed his head. "I appreciate your generosity, but your head is already highly priced for his majesty."

"He will not know. I can arrange for a withdrawal from my personal treasury. All you need to do is ask."

"Daughter of Dokeianos." the Emperor stated loudly. "Remove yourself from my presence, since you continue to be obnoxiously social with my guest."

Anna stood silently and nodded toward Ragnvaldr. She nodded at the Norman, and then removed herself from the *Kathisma.*

Storming back to her apartments, Anna entered her foyer in tears. Ragnvaldr followed as always, but kept his distance as the lady wept.

"I want to go home," she sobbed. "I want … I want my husband here. I want our lives back. I want this evil imposter of an Emperor to ..."

"Shh ..." Ragnvaldr hissed. "That's enough of that. You're stronger than this."

"I can't do it anymore. I cannot. His uncle never treated me like this! What have I done to deserve this treatment?"

"Aside from opening your mouth, you are on two days with no sleep. You need to rest. Your face is exhausted and your words are not becoming of you. Look at you!" Ragnvaldr put his axe against the wall and took Anna to her bedroom and put her in front of a large silver mirror.

"That is the weakness of a woman, not the strength of an Imperial Lady of Rome."

Anna looked at herself in the mirror, her face was reddened by the tears, but her darkened eyes gave her away.

"I can't sleep in here."

"Yes, you can. You will not be attacked here again. That would be foolish."

"But how do I know for sure?"

"I am here. You are safe."

"You will stay in here as I sleep?"

"If that is what my princess desires, then it will be so."

The Persian servant came into the bedroom and Anna sat down to have her take down her hair and undress to rest.

Ragnvaldr watched, and the servant became uneasy, "My lady … This man ..."

"He is to stay in here. I will rest in my tunic."

Anna's hair was long, but it was often disguised very differently in tight nets and heavy plates of precious metals and stones that weighed her down and framed her face. As soon as her hair fell and the servant brushed it, it was immediately put into a braid for sleeping. After her hair was dressed, she stood and faced her guard.

"You will stay here? As long as I rest?"

"You have my word." And took the chair she was seated on, and pulled it toward the wall for him to sit on.

"Samira." Anna spoke to her servant.

"Yes?"

"Make sure that my guard is refreshed. Bring him wine and fruits while I rest."

"As you wish."

Anna moved toward her bed and slid onto it gently. As soon as she did, she felt her exhaustion take hold almost immediately, and laid back with a soft sigh.

"Sleep well," Ragnvaldr said, as he watched her drift off.

Anna awoke when night had fallen on the Capital. Looking over at her guardsman, she found him as expected: sleeping deeply in his chair, with the empty cup of wine beside him. Smirking to herself, she slid out of bed, and began to put her plan in motion.

Dressing herself in as much as she could on her own, she wrapped herself in a dark cloak, and went to her doors. The night watchmen were at their posts, and jumped as she exited. Before they could say anything, bags of gold fell at their feet, and they remarkably stayed silent. Anna was now only a few steps away from her freedom.

She rushed through the Boukoleon Palace through unguarded, private walkways out onto a main thoroughfare on the palace grounds, and out onto the street to the south of the Hippodrome, which was eerily silent compared to what it was just hours earlier. There, she met a man, whom she had arranged through her servants to wait for her without anyone knowing, offered her passage on his carriage to the walls. There, she would wait until dawn, when she could bribe her way onto a caravan exiting the Gate of the Spring, and leave Constantinople forever.

A sense of deep relief washed over her as she watched the Great Palace grow distant from her with every step the horses took, and it took almost two hours for her to reach the great complex of walls surrounding Constantinople. The most advanced system of defense in the world, and amazingly beautiful with their layers of stone and brick, the walls of Theodosius were a marvel to behold, and impenetrable by attacking forces. She paid the man for his passage and slid off the cart, then began heading toward the embattlement where she would hide until daybreak, but someone stepped in her way.

She went to walk around the figure, but he grabbed her wrist.

"No!" she yelled, and looked up to see Ragnvaldr looking down at her.

"No ..." she shook her head. "Please no … don't take me back … Please."

"You drugged me."

"I had to."

"How long have you had this planned?"

"Since yesterday. I can't live as a prisoner, no matter how golden my jail is."

"You could have simply asked me to go with you, instead, you have your handmaiden slip me a sleeping draught in wine. After saving your life just days ago, you mean to flee without any protection? Thankfully I woke up and Samira told me where you were headed. I followed the cart the minute it left the palace. Do you have any idea what could have happened to you? Have you gone mad?"

She looked up at him, into those blue eyes. "I was desperate and not thinking…I…I will not put you in any more danger. You have done enough for me, Varangian."

"Ragnvaldr. The name, please, is Ragnvaldr."

Carts rushed past the couple to head toward the gate, and Anna was nearly clipped. Ragnvaldr grabbed her and pulled her close against him to avoid the traffic further, but his hold became more of an embrace, which Anna reluctantly rolled free of.

"We need to get out of here," Ragnvaldr said.

"Come," she said. "I know where we can go, and be safe."

She led him to a staircase that took them on top of the wall, in an embattlement lit only by a single torch. This part of the wall overlooked the countryside spreading out away from the city, which faded quickly into the darkness of night beyond the lower levels and moat of the impressive structure.

"Guards are only stationed near the gates. I learned that when I was young … I would often come here to escape. That is why I knew I would be safe here for a time," she whispered to him when they got up there.

Ragnvaldr turned and looked back at Constantinople, which still glittered at night with the light of hearths, torches and candles. In the distance, the Propontis and Golden Horn reflected these lights, as well as the light of the crescent moon.

"The City of Gold," he whispered. "I dreamed of it as a child. To see this as it was described to me when men would return with their riches either in trade or service to the Emperor. And now I am here."

"And I dream of seeing something else," Anna replied.

"You were not a happy bride."

Anna shook her head. "No. Love grew in time, but not at first. I was a lonely girl, across the waters from my home. I missed my shells and my sand and my dolphins, but I was born to be in the courts someday. I was to bring my dowry to my husband, and give my father's land to the Emperor."

"So the Emperor, he practically owns your life."

"Almost." Anna laughed to herself. "Sicily has since been taken by the Saracens and the Normans, but my father is safe there. He was actually born in a village on the other side of the Bosporus because his family left the island when the Saracens took Syracuse. He joined the armies as a boy and grew to become a powerful commander. When he was old enough to retire, he was granted land wherever he wished, and that was home in Sicily. After some careful purchasing and deals with the Saracens controlling Syracuse, he was able to secure the house of his ancestors and rebuild it. We were not the only Romans on the island, but my neighbors were Muslim. Mother came from the northern part of the island where the Normans inhabit, and married my father without fear. We had a safe home there, it was very difficult for me to leave."

"To be a woman born of nobility sounds like a…how do you say it? A bad idea?" Ragnvaldr stumbled on his translation.

"That is not a terrible way to put it, no." Anna replied with a smile.

"Where I come from, men are free," Ragnvaldr began. "And women. Our women farm with us, work with us, war with us; in fact, some of the women in my town were better fighters than the men! Though I did fight before, a few years ago, but I resigned and decided I'd much rather farm berries than fight against others."

Anna raised an eyebrow, "And yet…you're here? Why did you resign? I thought warriors are well revered in the Northern lands."

"They are." He began. "But I had lost much, and saw much I did not wish to see. Then Thorfinnr passed through my lands returning from *Miklagaard*, I mean, Constantinople before deciding to go back. He told me magnificent tales, and, after telling him of my previous service as a warrior in my village, he asked if I would go with him. I immediately declined. But, he pushed, and on his return urged me once again. Other than my farm, I owned no property of value, and I had no family to care for, just my seeds and horses used on the plow. As we looked over my grounds, frozen from the winter and unplanted. The sky was gray, the air was cold, and it wasn't terribly difficult for me to change my mind. Sweden is an icy, gray place, but I find myself often missing the snow and quiet."

Anna smiled. "I would like to see that someday."

Ragnvaldr stepped forward to her and took her hands. "No." He looked down, and brushed one of his fingers along her palms. "These hands are that of a lady, of a woman, unlike any woman in the North. They are soft, and untouched by labor or chapped by the cold. These hands are that which belong to a woman who should never see the harshness of true labor or the lives of the poor. Women of the North would mock you for your softness."

"And what of the men?" Her voice became lower.

"Men long for the touch of soft hands ..." He whispered back, and brought Anna's hands to his face. He closed his eyes and took in the scent of her rich perfume as it wafted up from her wrists.

Anna's breathing became labored, but she didn't struggle. Instead, she moved in closer, close enough to where he could feel the warmth of her words against his neck, and she could feel the warm of his face beneath her fingers.

"They will kill us if they catch us."

Ragnvaldr opened his eyes then, only enough to meet her own, "Then I will die a blissful man, knowing that on my last night, I held in my arms, a princess."

Their lips met. Gently at first, but with each passing moment, each kiss grew with passion. Noises were heard below which drove the two apart; it was the changing of the guard, and Imperial soldiers would be moving through the ramparts to their stations. That meant that dawn was dangerously near, and the couple needed to act quickly.

Anna was quiet, and motion for Ragnvaldr to follow as she ducked down from the embattlement. Once they were both down on the grass, Ragnvaldr gently pulled Anna into a shadow to steal another kiss, but she skulked around quickly, and beckoned him yet again. She led him along the barrier of the wall, and into an alcove within a church corridor out of the sight of passers-by. This continued for the duration of the distance back to the Boukoleon: swiftly moving between structures silently as to not disturb the sleeping city, stealing kisses and touches, no matter if it was monastery or marketplace. It was like a game, a dangerous game of hide and seek that could result in serious consequences if caught.

Perhaps driven by fear, or just their emotions, the time it took to return to the Boukoleon seemed to be halved than it was to reach the walls, and they had made it safely into Anna's bedroom before sunrise.

CHAPTER 4
NIGHT AND DAY

Samira entered her lady's chamber an hour after sunrise as was tradition, and released a scream of shock on seeing Anna in bed with her guardsman, both resting peacefully. She started swearing in a mixture of Greek and Persian while making constant signs of the cross and turning away.

Anna shot awake and sat up, which pulled some of the covers from Ragnvaldr, who grabbed at them quickly to hide his form from the servant.

"The hells?" he groaned, half asleep.

"My princess, you did not commit that sin!"

"My sins are not for you to grant me salvation from!" Anna shouted back at her servant. "You will speak of this to no one!"

"I ..." Samira stammered and leaned against the archway, continuing to look away from the bed.

"You will swear it on your grave, which I will bring you to early, if you as much as whisper of what you have seen."

Ragnvaldr shot up a salute from where he was laying on his back. "My lady!" he said, groggily and jokingly, and Anna batted down his arm.

"I swear it," Samira said softly.

"LOUDER."

"My lady, I swear it!"

"Good, now bring us some bread. Treat him as you would a prince as long as he is beside me."

"Yes, my lady."

After Samira ran off to bring food, Anna flopped back on her bed, and sighed heavily. Ragnvaldr gave a laugh, leaned over and kissed her on the shoulder gently before sitting up, and looking for his garments on the floor.

"Where are you going?" Anna sat back up.

"I shouldn't stay in here with you."

"But, you would have been in here, anyway."

"Oh, right." Ragnvaldr relaxed a bit, but still reached for his tunic. "She still doesn't need to see me unclothed."

Anna reached over and pulled Ragnvaldr back into the bed with her by his wrist. He gave no struggle and simply fell back so that his head was lying on her lap. He smiled and reached up to take some of her hair in his hands as it fell to the sides of her shoulders.

"We don't have to go anywhere," she said to him softly. "Relax. We are safe."

"As much as I believe you, flower, you know as much as I do that you will be expected somewhere outside of your room today, and I feel that wearing me as a robe is inappropriate."

Anna laughed. "Perhaps you are right." She leaned over and kissed his forehead.

Ragnvaldr sat up, and slid his tunic over his head. Anna almost protested that it was Samira's job to dress him as well, and realized that he wasn't used to that treatment, and remained silent as she grabbed for her own silk robe.

She watched him dress, and, knowing that the line had been crossed, reflected on how difficult it would be for them now. How outside of the walls of this bedroom, they had to go back to prisoner and guard, to nobility and commoner, to Roman and barbarian … Samira was right. It was a sin. Not just fornication, but also one of social graces. If anyone did find out, anyone of importance who cared little for Anna, Ragnvaldr would be killed and Anna would surely be exiled or, worse, killed as well.

Ragnvaldr knew this, too; he could tell by the expression of worry on Anna's face. By taking her to bed last night, he took a risk on her already-endangered life.

Samira returned to the bedroom with a loaf of bread and a jug of diluted wine, and refused to make eye contact with Ragnvaldr as she set up the breakfast table by the window with two chairs and cups instead of one. Before she could leave the room in silence, Anna grabbed her arm.

"Taste it," she demanded.

Samira sighed, and poured herself a sample of wine, which she drank, and then consumed a piece of bread for them as well.

"I will not kill you, or him, my lady." She poured them each their own glass of wine.

"You have yet to give me any reason to not trust you, Samira," Anna stated, as she broke herself off a piece of bread. "You have been my closest and most honest servant for many years now. I have cared for you and your family as if they were my own. I ask only for your support and silence in this matter."

"Your actions just startled me, my lady," Samira nodded. "I apologize for my outburst ... and for waking you too, my lord." She bowed toward Ragnvaldr.

"I am no lord," Ragnvaldr shook his head. "Just yesterday you called me Ragnvaldr, and today I ask that you do the same."

Samira nodded quietly and stepped out of the room in silence.

Anna didn't even look up, she continued eating her bread and sipping her wine to break her fast.

Ragnvaldr looked at her. He wasn't accustomed to the

noble way of life. He had watched it now for several months, sure, but to be treated as one and to watch how those of the lower classes were treated at this perspective was entirely different.

"It offends you not how you take your tone of voice with her?" he asked.

Anna looked up, confused. "I don't understand."

"You speak to her as if she is, well, lower."

"And?"

"Oh." Ragnvaldr realized what he had said. "Yet you said you cared for her as family."

Anna laughed. "I never even thought about it. I do not mistreat my help. They are paid well, clothed well and sheltered well."

"And do you care for them?"

"Yes. They are in my service for a reason. Ask Samira or her daughters, or her husband, who guards my door on day watch – they would work for no other."

"But there may be a day they are gone." Ragnvaldr leaned back. "Could you live without them?"

Anna paused. "I ... don't know."

Samira rushed in to the bedroom suddenly, her eyes as wide as her grin. "My lady! You have been freed!"

"What?" Anna blinked at the servant's sudden

outburst.

"Word has come – look!" She brought a piece of paper to her mistress, which Anna read for herself. "The Emperor is allowing you leave of your room and the palace as long as Ragnvaldr is with you!"

Anna smiled, and looked over at Ragnvaldr. "We shall go into the city, today!" She jumped to her feet. "To the markets, yes, the markets!"

Ragnvaldr, on the other hand, didn't seem as excited. "The streets? You will walk free in the streets of Constantinople the first chance you get to actually leave the palace and go shopping? After last night and now this, I do firmly believe that you are mad."

"Oh," Anna smirked, "I don't walk. Samira! Send for my chair men. We go in style, my darling! Come, I dress for the town!"

--

"You weren't kidding when you said that you didn't walk," Ragnvaldr said to her as they were preparing to exit the palace gates onto the city roads. He looked up at her, elevated on her whitewashed litter, carried by four Persian eunuchs, as the gates opened and they were able to face the public.

It was an unusual sight to see an Imperial woman exit the palaces, but Anna was always far more adventurous than her fellow courtiers. She smirked, but her face was almost entirely obscured by the dark red veil, trimmed in fine gold fringe, she had wrapped her body in to exit. Laws dictated that women needed to be covered outdoors, and Imperial ladies were no exception: they just made it look better.

Commoners scattered to the sides of the street as the litter came down toward the markets. Some bowed, not knowing who they were in the presence of, other than someone important. Some children waved, and Anna waved back, which got the young girls giggling in excitement that they had been noticed by a princess.

The main markets were not far from the palace district, but the crowds were starting to grow denser, and beggars were coming out to ask for aid from the noblewoman. She kept a purse of coins on the side of her person just for this occasion, and began flicking gold pieces toward those that seemed the neediest. Those that got too close to the litter had an armored Varangian to deal with, and they were fast to back off.

They arrived at a familiar merchant, who rushed out to see Anna as soon as he got word there was an Imperial was in the market.

"My lady! My lady!" he flagged her down. "My silks! Please, come in to see my silks!"

Anna motioned for the chair to be brought down, and Ragnvaldr immediately came to her aid to allow her to step off with ease. As the crowd gathered, the eunuchs suddenly turned into armed guards, and Anna was able to enter the shop in peace.

"Princess!" The shopkeeper knelt. "I always do so look forward to your patronage! Please, anything I can help you with?"

"This guard with me, he needs my colors," she ordered. "See to it that he gets only the finest stock of red and black in your private stores for the workshops. Actually, I will take the whole bolts."

Ragnvaldr looked at her. "You are buying for me?"

"If you are continuing to serve my house, you will wear my colors. This fine merchant supplies the Imperial workshops directly, so my orders are sent directly to the tailors." She walked along the rows of bolts of silk, and her eyes fell on a shimmering gold samite woven with medallions. "This as well!" she called out. "It shall be a new formal garment, and I will order it to be covered in pearls."

"At once, your Highness!" The merchant scrambled to write things down as he pointed for his porter to take the bolts from the shelves. "Is there anything else today? I have not seen you in some time; I was wondering if you were going to return after ..."

Anna raised a hand to silence him from speaking of the death of her husband. "I am here now, that is all that matters."

"Indeed, my Princess, and your patronage is always greatly appreciated. It honors me greatly to know that the Imperial family themselves come directly to me for their fine garments. Though I fear with the Emperor's new taxes on fabric, the common folk such as me will not be able to afford my wares, which could be disastrous."

Anna sighed; there was little she could do to overturn any laws – that was done by the Emperor and occasionally the senate directly.

"If he would listen to me, I would share my thoughts about his taxes, however, this for now is the best I can do." She reached into her purse and pulled out several gold coins and handed them to the merchant.

His eyes were wide, and he shook his head. "My Princess, this is way too much for your bill."

"It's for you, and your business." She made sure his hands closed around the coins. "I won't take it back, so don't even plead. Put it into a safe place: should your business fail, you have savings."

"Your Highness is most generous." He fell to his knees, gripping the coins and looking up at her. "If only you could have been our Augusta."

"It doesn't work like that, I'm afraid," Anna smiled. "Now please stand. You know I dislike that greatly."

The silk seller stood slowly, and nodded at Anna before retreating into his shop further to hide the large sum of money.

Ragnvaldr smiled a bit. "Are we ready, my princess?"

"Yes, onward we go to the next shop!" She smiled widely, and Ragnvaldr assisted her toward the litter, but a woman came through and pushed the Varangian aside, causing Anna to almost tumble to the ground; but she caught herself, and she was soon surrounded by the sword-wielding chair-carriers.

The woman tried to tackle Ragnvaldr, but he repelled her with ease, and then held his axe out in front to keep her back.

She was tattered, dirty, and appeared to be pregnant. As soon as the blades were pointed at her, she simply started laughing, and speaking in a language that was completely beyond Anna's knowledge.

Common folk suddenly surrounded the litter, wondering who in their right mind would have the wherewithal to attack an Imperial, especially one with a Varangian by her side.

"What is she saying?" Anna demanded. "Can anyone understand her?"

Ragnvaldr stared at the woman, who spat at the ground near his feet, and he just tightened the grip on his axe and shook his head at her.

"Just some beggar, your Highness. Nothing more."

"I see," Anna said, reaching into her pouch and pulling out three gold coins. "Here," she said, tossing them at the woman's feet. "Get out of here; otherwise I would have you arrested for your behavior."

The woman dove on the coins, looked back at the princess, then at Ragnvaldr, laughed and ran off into the crowd.

Ragnvaldr turned back to face Anna and said, plainly, “You should not have done that.”

“She obviously needs help.”

“She should be arrested for assaulting you,” Ragnvaldr sneered.

Anna stepped onto the chair, looking at her guard and lover, and simply said, as the eunuchs raised her, “It's important to understand that those of lower standing are still standing, and need to remain standing.”

She tapped the side of the chair, and said, “We return to the palace. That was enough excitement for one afternoon.

They found themselves in bed again soon after arriving back in her apartments, and napped quietly in each other's embrace, exhausted from the day’s events, but mostly the long night before.

A caller came at the doors, then, and Samira’s husband entered.

He announced, “A Varangian here to see the guardsman!”

Ragnvaldr, heard this, and rushed to dress as fast as he could, before rushing out of the bedroom and into the foyer, where his messenger was waiting at the door.

“Haakon, what is it?” he asked in Norse.

"Thorfinnr is summoning you to the barracks, as soon as you ... are ready." He looked down at Ragnvaldr's bare feet and unbelted tunic. "You smell of a lady's perfume."

"I was assisting the princess in ..."

"I don't care, Ragnvaldr. Just don't keep the commander waiting."

Haakon turned and left with no further words and Ragnvaldr returned to the bedroom where Anna now awake and eavesdropping behind the arch into the foyer.

"I'll get dressed," she said when he entered.

"You ... are coming with me to the barracks?" Ragnvaldr looked at her as if she had six heads.

"You can't leave my side, as ordered." She shrugged and rang a bell for Samira to come in and assist her to dress. "I guess that means I can't leave yours."

Ragnvaldr smiled and grabbed her forcefully for a kiss just as the servant walked in, and walked right back out.

--

They arrived at the barracks of the Varangian guard within an hour's time, once Anna was dressed to leave. Ragnvaldr led the princess into a common area where most of the off-duty guard were resting and conversing, but the presence of an Imperial made them all jump to their feet and suddenly silence themselves.

"At ease, good men, I am not here for ceremony," she said, but few men relaxed, realizing that the room was in no shape to entertain a lady, let alone an Imperial, and several rushed to pick up belongings and refuse that were strewn about.

The place was a collection of artifacts and furnishings from the North that made the men less homesick. Ornately carved chairs and various other decorations spotted the room, interspersed with more local décor, including silk drapery and upholstery. Some men were working on projects right there, including sewing and embroidering their own tunics to better fit the style of their people, and lacing together their issued lamellar armor.

Conversations that did continue to take place were from a variety of dialects of the Northern tongue that Anna was not familiar with; she strained to listen, and did manage to pick up bits and pieces.

"Thorfinnr." Ragnvaldr stepped toward the commander. "You called for me?"

Thorfinnr was seated and speaking to a compatriot beside him when turned his gaze forward and saw Anna with Ragnvaldr, and blinked. "My lady, what are you doing here? This is no place for you."

"Ragnvaldr cannot leave my side," she replied. "He is simply obeying orders by bringing me here."

Thorfinnr rolled his eyes. "Sit," he said, standing from his own chair and giving it to her. "I will not have you standing when comfort is to be had." He took her hand and led her toward the chair. "Somebody bring our guest a fine drink!"

"This is all highly unnecessary, Thorfinnr. You know this," she said, reluctantly sitting.

"You know as well as I do that one of the Greeks can come in and see you in here, we may as well provide you with proper hospitality." A very blond guard brought him a ceramic cup, and Thorfinnr handed it to Anna. "Please, drink. Allow us to serve you."

Anna took a sip of the beverage, anticipating wine, and pulled back quickly. "It's so sweet!" she winced. "What is this? You drink this regularly?"

The men laughed.

"We call that mead, my lady," Thorfinnr smiled. "It is our wine. From honey." He turned to the men that were resting around the hall. "Entertain our guest while I have words with Ragnvaldr. She knows some of our words, and will enjoy seeing your crafts."

Various warriors stood up to visit the princess, bringing with them their projects or other goods they wish to show to her, as they were not used to an Imperial showing even the slightest interest in their culture. They showed her embroidery, carvings, and brought her more bottles of their brewed honey drink for her to taste, to see if they would like theirs more than the others.

Thorfinnr took Ragnvaldr to the side and away from the earshot of Anna, and said softly, "I am leaving Constantinople."

"What?" Ragnvaldr was surprised. "You're leaving? You can't leave – you're our commander!"

Thorfinnr motioned for him to keep his voice down, and glanced back at Anna, who was still thoroughly distracted by the other Varangians giving her gifts; she was now wearing several strands of glass beads around her neck and continuing to drink the mead.

He turned back to Ragnvaldr. "The Norman lord, he has offered me a position with his keep in Andalusia, and Tiernan too. We have freed the Armenian from the Hippodrome as well and our ship leaves at dawn."

Ragnvaldr was silenced. His best friend, the man who urged him to come and serve the Emperor, was now leaving.

"Ragnvaldr ..." Thorfinnr put a hand on his shoulder and moved in closer. "I want you to take charge here." He looked back at Anna. "And take care of her. I have known her since she was no more than a young bride, she deserves to be safe, and ..." He paused. "You smell of a perfume."

Ragnvaldr's expression changed, and his eyes instinctively shot to Anna, who had paused for a moment to look up and give him a soft smile. Thorfinnr caught this.

"Oh." His eyes widened. "Oh Ragnvaldr, that is a serious offense you commit."

"I refuse to stay away from her now, even if it is both

of our deaths." Ragnvaldr looked at her longingly for a moment, and then back at Thorfinnr. "No ... No, take her with you, Thorfinnr. Take her away from this place. She tried to escape last night and I caught her at the wall near the Gate of the Spring."

"I don't think I can," Thorfinnr replied. "When one is born to privilege, Ragnvaldr, they must live their lives as such. It is as I told you before: she may be wealthy and beautiful, but her job is to be used as a marriage contract to gain more lands and more money, and to have children to do the same. Right now, this experience I have given her to allow the men to speak with her and give her things, is the farthest she will ever get from that life. She knows this, which is why she embraces this moment so.

"I will ask you again, to let her go. She is more than a prisoner of the Emperor in your care, Ragnvaldr – she is also a prisoner of her own life."

As Thorfinnr spoke, Ragnvaldr's eyes watched Anna as she spoke with the other Northmen, seeing how she so starkly contrasted against them. Was she truly excited to be waited on by foreigners? Or were the foreigners just elated to be in the casual presence of an Imperial? Perhaps it was both? It was difficult to say.

"Ragnvaldr," Thorfinnr interrupted his thoughts. "I need you to stay here. These men need you."

"I am not a leader," he replied. "But her ..." He motioned toward Anna. "She, she is like an ambassador." And then it hit him. "That's it!" He threw his hands on Thorfinnr's shoulders.

“What? What’s it?”

“Her chance to leave! We can get her out of here! She can be an ambassador!”

Thorfinnr sighed, and slid his friend's hands from his shoulders. “Ragnvaldr ... she’s a woman. Woman here are not ambassadors. They’re marriage bait.”

Ragnvaldr sighed. “I'm beginning to understand this culture less and less.”

At that moment, before Thorfinnr could speak, Anna hiccupped, and then the entire group broke out into a fit of laughter.

“By the gods ...” Thorfinnr winced. “How much have they given her?”

“She is not used to the drink.” Ragnvaldr looked over at her, noticing her flushed cheeks. “They dilute their wine.”

Thorfinnr was already walking back to the chair. “My lady,” he began. “Are you all right, child?

“I'm fine!” Anna laughed a bit, her neck dripping with strands of carved amber and lamp-worked glass. “This one, it tastes of berries!” She lifted the cup, which was mostly empty.

“Congratulations, men.” Thorfinnr rubbed his eyes. “You got a princess drunk.”

And with that, the barracks cheered.

"To drink in excess, is a sin!" Anna began to stand, but it was a wobbly, sloppy attempt, and Thorfinnr held her still. "Why do I feel this way? My head feels unclear and my body warm and relaxed."

"The mead is a stronger brew than your wine, Princess." he said softly. "I'm afraid for you it takes far less to feel the spirits than it is for my men and me. You are not used to it."

Anna laughed again and patted Thorfinnr on his arm, where he held onto hers firmly. "You're a good friend, Thorfinnr."

"As you are also, my princess."

"I don't like being a princess."

"Neither do I." He motioned for Ragnvaldr. "Bring her back to her chamber to rest this off."

"I'm going to miss you," Anna said softly, gripping Thorfinnr tightly.

He looked down at her. "You heard?"

She responded with a nod.

"Child ... I will miss you as well." Thorfinnr pulled her into an embrace. "To think out of my two decades of service to the Emperors, I have known you for seventeen years. You were but a scared girl then, and now, you are a woman. I was there for your marriage, and stood guard at the door the day you gave birth to your son, and heard his first cries. Now he is grown and wed, himself. The time has flown at a speed indescribable by words in both of our languages. I could have loved you as a daughter, but you adopted me as a true friend – a bond that does not often happen between Romans and Northmen; so that, I value more than any love between family."

Anna found herself in tears. "Is there anything I can give you? Do you need a salary? Silks? What can I do to make your journey comfortable and safe?"

"I will take nothing from your hands," Thorfinnr said in an insistent voice, taking her by her shoulders.

"Then take these from my ears." She reached up and removed from her lobes a pair of solid gold enameled earrings dripping with perfectly shaped teardrop pearls. "For all those times you listened when others would not. For the nights you would tell great stories of the North to entertain my son and I when my husband would travel, and for being there and doing more than any hired soldier should ever do for his employer. If asked, I will never say less than a respectful word about you and your kin of the North. You have earned my gratitude for the rest of my life."

"*Kyria* Anna." He bowed. "Your mind may not wish you to be a princess, but the words of your heart speak like that of an Augusta."

"Go with God," she whispered.

"Go, and greet the day," he responded in kind, before walking off in solitude from the barracks and his men, as he prepared to leave Constantinople forever.

As Ragnvaldr walked the staggering Anna back to the Boukoleon, it was clear her behavior was attracting the attention of others in passing, so Ragnvaldr pulled her down a small corridor, where her giggles were amplified by echoes. He motioned for her to quiet, but she instead put her arms around his shoulders.

"Kiss me," she demanded.

Ragnvaldr blinked. "But ... someone may see."

"Nobody is around ..." Anna looked from side to side. "No one comes down this hall."

Ragnvaldr attempted to protest, but Anna took his face in her hands, leaned up and kissed him passionately, which he did not refuse. After that kiss broke, they both laughed lightly and began kissing again, stopping only to breathe and laugh as Anna backed into a wall and Ragnvaldr pinned her there.

"My, what have we here?" A voice spoke out of the silence.

The kissing couple broke apart as soon as they heard him, and Anna looked away from the direction of the voice.

"Dear Anna Dokeianina." Steps came forward. "Is that you, my sister?"

Anna winced and turned her head back slowly, bringing into focus a figure that was unfortunately familiar.

"Maxentios Komnenos," she sneered. "My husband's charming brother. It's been ages."

Ragnvaldr felt his face grow hot. This could be bad. Very, very bad.

Maxentios smiled. "I see you're doing well for yourself. I'm glad to see that my brother's death didn't destroy your libido."

Ragnvaldr reached for his sword, but Anna stayed his hand.

"Well, Max. I'm pleased to see that there are no hard feelings." She smiled, but it was curt, and faded as she looked over his clothing. "*Megas Domestikos*? Who did you have to pleasure to get that position?"

"*Megas Domestikos*?" Ragnvaldr interrupted.

"Indeed." Maxentios adjusted his fine silk uniform. "Commander-in-chief of the armies; and I pleasured no one, dear sister – I earned it."

"Max is the youngest born to my husband's family," Anna said to Ragnvaldr. "He had no inheritance so he went to serve in the armies. Always has been a stirrer of pots."

"Are you speaking Barbaric?" Maxentios blinked. "I always knew you were a rare breed of stupid. Who is he? A Varangian? You're fucking a Northman now?"

Ragnvaldr moved, but Anna stepped forward before he could act at all. "You will hold your tongue of such words in the presence of an Imperial princess."

"You're no princess," Maxentios snorted. "You're nothing more than a lady with a good dowry and fertile hips from an island we don't even hold anymore."

"You speak like a swine."

"At least I don't sleep with one."

"Depends – when was the last time your wife bathed?"

Max was silenced for a few moments. "I can't say what I wish to say to you, and still be a follower of Christ."

"Every time you open your mouth, you blaspheme the Lord," Anna retorted. "And I don't just mean with words."

She turned, and noticed that Ragnvaldr was gone, and nowhere immediately in sight. This startled her visibly, and Maxentios laughed.

"So much for your faithful guard, *princess*," he chided.

"Oh, how I wish I could trust you," Anna grimaced, and then ran off to find Ragnvaldr, fearing that if she was seen alone, it could be both of their heads.

CHAPTER 5
BROKEN HEARTS

Arriving back at her apartments, she frantically searched for Ragnvaldr, wondering why he would just disappear rather than defend her honor. She was confused and upset over the encounter with her brother-in-law, in addition to still being somewhat intoxicated; she found her way to her bed and threw herself upon it, where she caught her breath.

The room was spinning from the mead, and she closed her eyes and gripped the corners of the mattress as if it in some way would assist her in recovering. She eventually dozed off for what felt like hours, hearing the birds and waves outside of her bedroom window from the sea.

"Anna ..." Ragnvaldr's voice spoke softly from the archway.

She woke immediately. "There you are!" She shot up and ran to him. "I searched all over; I feared the worst ... Maxentios seeing us could be devastating."

Ragnvaldr looked down at the Roman woman with

cold eyes, and stepped back as she reached for him.

"Anna," he began. "I need to have words with you."

"About what?"

"I am resigning as your guard."

"What? You can't!"

"No. We can't go on like this. I can't endanger you further. I ... I can't. Not after today. In the market with ..." He paused. "With that woman, and just now with the Grand Domestic. Our lives are at stake for the sake of a love we cannot have. I will find a replacement for myself, and ... and you and I will continue as we were before last night." His voice was remarkably firm, but soft. "I'm sorry." The conflicting emotions in his eyes were giving him away, but the words were spoken.

Anna stood there, feeling as if something blunt had been forced through her chest. Her face grew pale, and her eyes widened.

"I ... I don't understand," she said in barely a whisper. "Why? I ... I thought ..."

"It was nothing, Anna," Ragnvaldr interrupted. "I let my passion take hold of me when I should not have. It was just one night, anyway." His voice grew stronger.

"You're just saying this because of ..."

"No. No, I'm not just saying it." He backed away. "There is nothing. I feel nothing. It was steps that we should not have taken. You are just a lonely old woman, but you have a marriage coming up. You'll be fine. I will still be here in the service of the Emperor if you need anything before you're dragged away to France for property and babies." The back of his throat tightened as he deliberately inflicted pain on her, somehow knowing that this was the only way.

Anna was taken aback, and as she felt the heat in her eyes beginning to build, she acted impulsively, and brought her hand upon the Varangian's cheek with an incredible force driven by raw emotion. The slap moved his face, and brought Anna's body around in almost a full half-circle, even heavily laden in her clothing as she was.

"Get out."

Ragnvaldr immediately brought a hand to his face where she had struck him. Light scratches from her rings were causing his face to sting and redden rapidly.

"Anna ... I'm ..."

"Who are you to speak to me in such an informal manner?!" she shouted at him, her tone completely changing, unlike in any way he had seen previously. "How dare you speak my first name, you lowly barbarian! Have you no training to be in the service of the Empire?"

If her strike didn't sting enough, her words were like saltwater in his wounds. It was like the sun had set on the brightness that was once her radiance, with nothing more than those sentences. She truly was one of them: decorative, authoritative, and if the sudden fiery hatred in her eyes told any story, cold-hearted.

"Your Imperial Highness," he corrected himself, eyes closed. "I will take my leave now."

He bowed deeply, avoiding eye contact, and left the bedroom. Anna ran after him and watched him gather his belongings from his sleeping quarters. His armor, his tunics, his trousers...everything that he had moved in with the weeks prior was gathered together in a satchel. Bag over one arm and large axe in the other, while wearing his full resplendent suit of bronze lamellar armor, Ragnvaldr walked past Anna with a silent bow and left the apartments without another word spoken.

As the doors closed behind him and the light from the main hall was squelched from Anna's view, she dropped to her knees, and began to weep loudly as if he could hear her from beyond the heavy wood and stone. Despite what she visualized, the doors did not reopen. Ragnvaldr did not come back in and sweep her off her feet – no. She was trapped for good now, in her prison of marble, stone, and other meaningless luxuries.

Some of her attendants came and attempted to get her from the floor, but she refused and remained sitting in a heap of silk and linen. The mead had left her with a headache, and she felt as if the walls around here were moving. As far as she knew from these reactions, she was going mad. Eventually she succumbed to the tugs of the servants, and allowed herself to be brought to bed.

Ragnvaldr arrived back at the barracks, and the men watched as he silently brought in all of his belongings to where his bunk was. His eyes were fixed on the ground, and his expression defeated.

"Haakon," he said. "Go and see to the princess. Make sure that she is protected and controlled under the terms of her house arrest."

"But ... Ragnvaldr ..." Haakon stood. "Why?"

"As your new commander, do as I say," was the reply.

Thorfinnr had not fully vacated yet, and approached Ragnvaldr as he removed his clothing from the satchel and placed it in a chest near his bed.

"What are you doing back?"

"You know what I'm doing back."

"No, actually, I don't."

Ragnvaldr resigned with a sad sigh. "I had to leave her. Today was unnerving and dangerous. My affections would simply be her undoing."

"Is she all right?" Thorfinnr's face was concerned.

"No." Ragnvaldr slammed the chest shut. "No, she is not all right." He pointed to the ring-shaped bruises and cuts on his cheek.

Thorfinnr sighed. "You must learn to be gentle with women, otherwise they will not be gentle with you."

"I had no choice." Ragnvaldr removed his helmet. "The Grand Domestic ... he ..."

"The Grand Domestic did what?" That same familiar voice appeared in the doorway to the dormitory wing.

Thorfinnr stood at attention rapidly, and Ragnvaldr reluctantly fell into place.

Maxentios approached them slowly, inspecting other members of the guard who were also present in the room as he passed and spoke, pompously. "The Grand Domestic saw an extreme violation of code today. The Grand Domestic saw the dear wife of his deceased brother being taken advantage of by nothing more than a hired barbarian. The Grand Domestic," he stopped in front of Ragnvaldr, "could have you killed for such actions."

Ragnvaldr swallowed hard, but didn't speak. Maxentios, aside from being commander of the Imperial land armies, was akin to second-in-charge under the Emperor. The wrong words meant death, which, at this point, could very well be inevitable.

"Gentleman, we have a problem!" Maxentios turned to the barracks as a whole. "The war on the border to the north grows worse. Despite the marriage of Prince Alexander to the Bulgarian princess and his presence in the country as an ambassador in negotiations for land, some troops in Bulgaria have refused to stand down, and they continue to press on. The situation is becoming dire, as we need to move more men to the south to aid in the fortification of Antioch. Men of the Varangian Guard, it is time you're put to good use. You're being sent to war."

Ragnvaldr blinked a few times. "War," he thought. "I didn't sign up for this."

Maxentios continued, "As many of you know, we count on the men of the Varangian Guard to enter a battle at its peak, and obliterate the enemy in as little time as possible. We need this conflict to come to an end, and quickly. As we divert supplies and assistance to the fight against the Turks, we need these Bulgarians to accept that we've won. Your job is to go in, shut them down, and be home in time for supper in less than a month's time.

"I have a list of men who will be joining me on the campaign north; the rest will remain here and continue to serve the Imperial family and His Imperial Majesty howsoever they see fit."

He pulled a folded piece of parchment from his belt, opened it, and threw it on top of a bed.

"There are your names. If you cannot read Greek, Thorfinnr will translate. If your name appears on the list, then you are to gather your armor and a cart of provisions and meet me at the Hippodrome tomorrow morning to depart. I so look forward to watching you heathens at work. That is all."

Maxentios turned, shot Ragnvaldr one final glance and then walked out of the barracks as fast as he entered.

As soon as he was gone, Ragnvaldr walked over to the parchment with Thorfinnr, and looked down at the foreign language.

"Well?" he asked.

Thorfinnr looked over the writing, squinting and trying

to process the Greek alphabet slowly.

"Yes," he said glumly. "Ragnvaldr Gunnarsson. You're at the top of the list."

"Damn him." Ragnvaldr looked up toward the door the Grand Domestic had exited through. "He did it on purpose."

"It could be worse. He could have simply had you killed."

"I think that's still the plan; this is just an easier way for him to get away with it."

--

Anna was lying on her bed. Her brown locks were completely down and relaxed around her head and shoulders, and she was stripped down to the lightest linen smock she had. Samira was carefully running a hand through her lady's hair, and applying a cool, damp cloth to her face to soothe her, but Anna's tears continued, and her eyes were swollen and reddened with her sadness.

Samira's husband came into the bedroom and bowed. "My princess, your new guardsman is here."

"Does he have a name?" Anna muttered. "I do not want any of them which I do not know."

"It's Haakon." The familiar Varangian stepped in, removing his helmet and smiling lightly. "You know me, your Highness. I have been here for many years."

Anna lifted a hand to wave half-heartedly.

"Are you ill, dear Princess?" He asked.

"The lady is exhausted and dizzy from the drink that was given to her at the barracks," Samira spoke up. "She will be well again tomorrow."

"I see," Haakon nodded. "Well, I'll just step out here, then, as to not disturb her rest." He turned to leave, but sighed and looked back. "He insisted that I do not tell you, but the Grand Domestic is deploying guards to Bulgaria. Ragnvaldr is going with them."

Anna shot up, nearly throwing poor Samira from the bed.

"Bulgaria? What is going on in Bulgaria?" Panic was in her voice. "My son! What is happening?"

Samira gently forced her back down onto the bed. "My lady, please relax ..."

Anna raised a hand and swatted away her attendant.

Haakon continued, "We are having struggles maintaining peace at the border as the armies are being moved to defend against the Turks. As far as I know, the Prince Alexander is safe."

Anna fell back onto her pillow, and began to sob again. Samira rolled her eyes and put the cloth over her mistress' face.

"This is why you do not tell women of military campaigns." Thorfinnr stepped in behind Haakon. "All it does is trouble them of their husbands and sons." He approached the bedside with little decorum. "You really are in a sad state, aren't you, child?"

"How dare you speak to her like that!" Samira frowned.

Thorfinnr just waved her off.

"I assure you, Samira," Anna grumbled from under the cloth, "he has called me worse in my youth."

"Old age has made you a crybaby." Thorfinnr sat on the edge of the bed and helped himself to a plate of fruit on a table nearby.

"I thought you were leaving."

"I said tomorrow morning. I don't own much; I just have a lot of saved wages that will be difficult to carry."

"Now you know why rich people have slaves, dear friend."

"Indeed." He bit into the fruit, and spoke while chewing. "But enough about our amassed wealth. I came to check on you."

"I must look like death," Anna replied.

"No, you look very much alive, and I pray that a fair lady as yourself never sees death again."

"Yet I am given news that my son and my supposed-now-former lover are being surrounded by battle."

"I cannot speak for your son or his safety, and I wish I

could. I can say, though, that this action was taken just today by the Grand Domestic. I knew nothing of it, or I would have not left Ragnvaldr in charge suddenly like this."

Anna snarled at the mention of her brother-in-law. "I don't have the power to override anything he commands."

"Would you if you could?" Thorfinnr asked carefully.

Anna nearly whispered in reply. "No. The Empire must be protected."

"Then you must take this." Thorfinnr pulled from his belt a sheathed sword, and threw it on the bed between them.

Anna sat up to look at it, and then looked back up at the Varangian.

"What do you expect me to do with that?"

"Preferably, stick it into someone who deserves it."

"Ladies do not touch swords." She relaxed back onto the bed, her face ridden with disgust over the weapon beside her.

"Ladies, maybe not." Thorfinnr stood. "But, occasionally, a lonely girl I knew once, did."

"I can't remember how to fight." She reached up and held the damp cloth over her eyes.

"You will, when the time comes for you to." He walked toward the head of the bed, and pulled the cloth from Anna's face. "Once upon a time, there was a girl who came from far away to marry a prince who paid no attention to her. Her only friends were group of young foreign soldiers ten years older than her, who taught her how to hold her own with a sword and axe because it was their idea of fun, until she was taken away, forced to dress in purple, and behave like a stuck-up piece of jewelry. Pretty to look at, cold and sharp to the touch, but gold can still melt. In time the girl grew up into a woman, and when the prince died ..." he pulled the blanket from her body, which made the servants gasp, but Anna simply sat up, with an angry expression, and took hold of the sword.

Thorfinnr smirked. "And when the prince died, she ran away from her problems instead of facing them, so when she did come back, they doubled, and she found herself locked in her room with a man she thought she could love because he was the first to give her any kind of affection ..."

Anna drew the blade, and held it at ready. Her tears had stopped, but her eyes were still red, which, coupled with the sword, made her look frighteningly fierce.

"So when that affection was taken away from her, all she could do was cry, like the spoiled ..."

Anna took a swing, but Thorfinnr was quick in drawing his other sword into a parry.

"Selfish ..."

Another swing and parry.

"Roman court brat that she was raised to be!"

Anna went in for a thrust, but Thorfinnr moved out of her path, and the weight of the sword carried Anna almost into the wall. She stumbled, but Thorfinnr caught her, and took the sword from her hand.

"Keep practicing, because women don't make it into the sagas by crying." He walked away from her, put the sword back into its sheath, and tossed it back on the bed. "Time for me to go."

Anna stood there, catching her breath and wiping tears from her eyes, glaring at the Varangian that had just completely embarrassed her.

"What are you running from, Thorfinnr?" She said , her voice broken with sobs, "I feel that I am not the only one who turned my back on problems."

Thorfinnr stopped to hear her words, but remained silent as he moved toward the door, and was met head on by an attendant just preparing to announce the visiting French duke to the princess.

"Oh," the attendant sneered at the Varangians and Persians in the same room with an ill, barely dressed Roman. "Is this a bad time?"

Thorfinnr stared down at the thin French man and his meager entourage, and then barked like a dog, which caused them to jump.

"I was just taking my leave," he said quietly, and then walked past them, without a proper goodbye.

--

Ragnvaldr looked over his pile of weaponry. From his signature long axe to his smallest sword, he stood there and stared at them on his bunk almost blankly. The heat of battle was on his mind now, not the woman he was with the night before, or any reflection of his belongings or homeland – just the prospect of war.

He had never seen true full war in years. Cutting down the occasional treasonous courtier or assassin, yes. Protecting his home village from a small intruding band, yes; but to go to the front lines, in armor, defending a country he knew little about for the sake of an oath and regular pay was an entirely foreign experience. He felt that no drills in the courtyard or polo fields would train him sufficiently for this. He thought only of his gods, and whom to pray to so that if he faces death at the enemy's hand, he would find his way into *Valhalla.*

A call came that the carts were rolling into the area of the barracks for loading. The guard would walk to Bulgaria, but their equipment would not. It was blatant which the Empire deemed to be more precious. It was days to the border, but they would have the luxury of taking a boat up the Euxine Sea for a fair portion of the trip to save their legs. They would need it.

It was almost morning.

"Ragnvaldr!" A call came from Thorfinnr as he walked through the dormitory with two porters carrying his goods to the waiting, Andalusia-bound ship.

Ragnvaldr turned and gave a smile. "May the gods protect you, my friend."

"And you as well," Thorfinnr replied. "Bring us glory."

"I will try," Ragnvaldr laughed. "Perhaps, in due time, I will meet you again in the Hall of *Valhalla*."

As Thorfinnr approached his friend's bunk, he looked down and noticed the elaborate necklace that was given to him two days prior by Anna. He reached down and took it gently in his hand, lifting it up to Ragnvaldr's eye level.

"Always wear a token a lady gives you."

"I desire not to."

"It will bring you fortune on the battlefield."

In response, Ragnvaldr snatched the medallion from Thorfinnr's hand, and put the chain over his neck.

"Always the superstitious one," Thorfinnr scoffed, smacking Ragnvaldr on the back, and continuing to walk by.

"What do I do?" Ragnvaldr asked, urgently.

"What do you mean?" Thorfinnr countered.

"At the border..."

"You fight, Ragnvaldr. You fight with every bit of fire in your soul." Thorfinnr looked back at him. "I would not have brought you here if I did not believe you could fight."

"I should not fear death," Ragnvaldr said softly.

"It is not death you fear," Thorfinnr smirked. "It's the pain you feel first." He turned back for a strong embrace, then, with one final smile, he hurried to the door. "I must go. Go and greet the day, Ragnvaldr!"

Ragnvaldr watched as his best friend disappeared into the rising sun's light through the corridor, and gathered his belongings to deploy.

Thorfinnr walked from the palace complex to a cart waiting outside. The Emperor ordered that the ship was not to dock in the city marinas, so it was to be waiting on the beach outside of the walls. Tiernan had already left before him, and was waiting on the shore just to the west of the Marble Tower where the boat was aground. It was a sight for sore eyes for any man from the north: with elegantly carved designs along the bow and stern, and larger than what was expected. It contrasted heavily against the smaller, more streamlined dromons normally seen around Constantinople.

The air was humid and thick in the Mediterranean summer morning, and the Norman lord was already aboard, overseeing the loading of the ship. The two Varangians walked onboard via a ramp on the soft wet sand. Thorfinnr paused and looked back toward the walled coastline of the city, and felt remorse immediately.

The Armenian Barabbas approached and stood beside

him, taking in the same scenery, and said, "I think I may miss this place after all."

Thorfinnr huffed, "Not so much the place, as the people."

"You fear for the princess' life."

"I fear for more than that." Thorfinnr turned and walked toward Patricius, who was giving the orders to shove off. "If I may request we made a stop."

The Norman turned and looked at the Varangian with a raised brow, "And that is?"

"Syracuse." Thorfinnr answered, "I have a dread feeling we may need to save a man's life."

--

The Varangians assembled in the Hippodrome shortly after first light, with the entire Imperial entourage overlooking them from the *Kathisma.*

The Emperor stood to speak, "Today, you barbarians will go and prove your worth to my Empire by doing something that needed to be done long ago. It's time we crush the Bulgarians along the border, and let them know that we are indeed, the strongest power in this part of the world. No longer will we continue to allow our own Romans to be butchered by nothing more than lowly Slavs. The time is now. We shall crush them!"

Ragnvaldr drifted off and his eyes instinctively found Anna among the ranks on the balcony. She stood out quite easily, wearing a veil of sheer red silk trimmed with thin gold strands that could be seen dancing as the soft morning wind and rising sun's light played with the rich fabric.

“Petals.” He thought to himself, “Petals that will wither and die.” For a moment he thought that their eyes met, but he wasn't sure, as their distance was great. Not that it mattered much anyway. She was wearing red, the color of blood. She knew as well as he did that death was inevitable at this point, be it hers, his, or both.

As they marched from the Hippodrome and to the port where they would catch their boats up the Euxine Sea to the border, all Ragnvaldr could remember of Anna now was that red shimmering veil. There was no face, no body, no perfume, just the colors, dancing in the wind. It was all he wanted to remember, if not less.

It was time for war.

CHAPTER 6
DIFFERENT WORLDS

Anna turned to leave from the *Kathisma,* and suddenly felt a strong hand grip on her upper arm. She turned to look for Haakon, but he wasn't in sight, and next to her was one of the Emperor's personal guards, a man who she was not familiar with. She was being led somewhere against her will, but before she could question or protest, doors opened to a private room just beyond the balcony, and she was handed immediately over to the Emperor himself. The room was closed behind them both, with nothing more than the light of several candelabras, and no guards to be found.

"You." He snarled in her face, "I've heard some nasty rumors about you."

Anna swallowed hard, "And what may those be, my Emperor?"

"That you disagree with the marriage proposal from the French duke!"

A wave of relief washed over her, but she wasn't out of the deep water yet, "I am able to make my own decisions in such matters!"

The Emperor reached forward and put his hand toward her breast, but brought it up and ran his fingers across the jeweled color of Anna's dalmatica. This caused her to immediately tense up and stand frozen in place.

"You do like red a lot…" he said, in a soft eerie tone.

"It is my favorite color." Anna responded quickly, still frozen out of the uncertainty of the situation.

"I always thought rubies were a fascinating stone." The Emperor continued, how they have such fire stuck inside of a small rock…glittering and reflecting light, such a passionate object, don't you agree?"

"Yes, my Emperor." Anna's voice cracked, and she grew warm. Sweat poured down her sleeves from under the weight of linen and silk onto her hands, which she clinched into shaking fists so tightly she should feel her fingernails cutting into her palm.

The Emperor traced his finger upward along Anna's neck and onto her face. She closed her eyes in reaction and he clinched her neck.

"Do not close your eyes in front of me!" He shouted in her face.

Anna winced again, but forced her eyes open, which made them easier to well up with tears, but she wouldn't let herself break down. The Emperor moved in closer, so that she could feel his hot breath against her neck.

"If only I knew you sooner…" He practically hissed, "If only I could have taken you as my bride instead of Stephanos, what an empress you would have made." He leaned in and gently kissed her neck, which caused every muscle in her body to stiffen.

"I would have been empress." Anna's tone changed

dramatically, "If you had been killed years ago and not allowed the option of exile." She wished that she had carried Thorfinnr's sword with her, for the words she spoke would surely anger him to strike at her.

Surprisingly, the Emperor did not act violently as Anna assumed he would, instead, he pulled back from her and laughed, "You're not a fool, Dokeianina. I expect nothing less from the woman whose father forced me to flee for France just days before you married my cousin. I have worked for nearly twenty years to get my dues, to be raised to the Purple, and I'd be damned if you, or any other person stood in my way."

"I could care less for the throne." Anna felt her nose wrinkle at the thought, "Men like you have left a bad impression on me."

"Ah, but did you not just say you would have been empress?" The Emperor contradicted, "Dearest Stephanos, the favorite of my dead uncle, your husband, as Emperor? A man equally dead and cold as the porphyry he lies in, is no Emperor."

"You killed him." Anna felt her eyes well up, "And your uncle. Poison…You said I am not a fool, Komnenos, and damnit, I know it was you!"

The Emperor smiled, the lines of his face looked sinister in the shadows cast by the candles, "No fool, indeed." He moved close to her again, and took her face in his hands. His brown eyes were black in the relatively dark chamber, but the madness was plainly visible. Leaning in, he gently placed a kiss on Anna's lips. She immediately pulled away from this without violent struggle, but he persisted until she finally gave in.

The kiss broke, and Anna turned her back to the

Emperor. Her bottom lip trembled out of shock or disgust of what she just allowed to happened, and she stared wide-eyed at the wall in front of her. The Emperor moved in and placed his hands on her shoulders tightly as he pushed his body against hers, forcing her red veil to be pinned between them, and her head to be brought back from its weight.

"The Duke leaves in three days' time." He whispered into her ear, "You have a choice. You will marry him, or, I can send my wife home with him after having our marriage annulled, and you can take his place at my side, in a position where you belong."

Anna trembled in his arms, but kept her ground. How was it that she gave into him so quickly if nothing but by pure fear?

"I need not an answer this very moment." The Emperor spoke into her ear again, "But I will need one soon. There is no third choice, Dokeianina. Well, there is, but I don't think it's what you want."

He let go of her and backed away, "Think on it carefully."

Anna uttered nothing and stood in place until she heard his footsteps reach the door and pass through it. Once the light of the door illuminated the room, she exhaled the breath she had been holding, closed her eyes as she gasped out of relief that he was gone. Turning around toward the door, Haakon was outside waiting for her, and she rushed toward him while pulling her red veil back over her shoulders and face to help hide her exasperation.

"My Lady, are you alright? I couldn't find you…I…"

"Just take me back home." She said sharply, and started walking hastily back toward the Boukoleon without him.

--

The Varangians landed at the Bulgarian border by nightfall of the next day. The Varangians were swift to arm themselves, unknowing what kind of ambush could await them in the dark along the front.

The Grand Domestic howled orders left and right, and Ragnvaldr ran with the rest of his men to the campsite for grouping. There, the rest of the Roman land army was awaiting them. They looked tired and battered, but the sight of reinforcements, especially the Northmen, was a pleasing one. To the army, it meant that the tables were finally going to turn on this engagement.

Throwing his gear on the ground, Ragnvaldr saw nothing past the line of tents and trees but darkness. The air was cool, but there was definitely a strong feeling of tension and strife on the fire dotted terrain of the soldiers' campsite. A few of the Greeks looked at him, but no words were spoken. Rest needed to be had so that battle could be fought tomorrow.

He walked over to the Grand Domestic's tent, where other commanders were meeting as well, and walked in with little adherence to decorum.

"What are we looking at?" He asked, interrupting the conversation of the highly decorated men.

"Ah yes, Barbarian," Maxentios smiled, "I was hoping you would join us. Gentleman, this is Ragnvaldr Gunnarsson, acting captain of the Varangian Guard. Have a seat, *Captain.*"

"I will stand." Ragnvaldr replied flatly, and looked down at the map on the table. "What is the plan?"

"All you need to do," Maxentios looked up at him, "Is come when we call. Like dogs to raw meat. Your men will come from behind our line, and shatter their defenses until they fall, or run home crying to their king. It's quite simple. This land is now ours; we simply need them off of it as efficiently as possible. The faster you do your job, the faster you go home to my dear sister."

"I care not for her. She was drunk and without her wits."

"You're not speaking back to me, are you, Barbarian?"

Ragnvaldr sighed, "No, sir."

"Good. Like I said, you will do what you told, come when you are called. Fight when we need you to fight, and that's that. Any questions?"

"No, sir."

"Be ready before dawn for a march. I advise you get sleep. No drinking."

"Yes, sir."

"Good, be gone with you."

--

In Constantinople, Anna sat silently in her bathtub, and watched as Samira poured another jug of hot, scented water into it. The aroma of jasmine and roses filled the air, and Anna's eyes were gazing off into the distance.

"My lady..." Samira put the jug on the floor, "Are you sure that you want to go through with this?"

"I have made my decision." Anna replied softly. "There is no other way."

"The tryst you had with that outlander has warped your senses these past few days." Samira took liberty to speak, "I feel that you were too soon a widow, and too soon to find a lover to sate your loneliness that you brought this pain upon yourself, and now, with the Emperor…"

"I have been alone most of my life, Samira." Anna interrupted, "I was the only child to a woman who died to bring a son to my father. Shunned in the court for my father's political views, married to a man who traveled most of his life and was ripped from me unfairly, stripped of my only son so that he could fit their mold, and locked in a gilded prison for slightly suggesting that the Emperor do something for himself."

"If I may speak freely..."

"You always do."

Samira sighed, "Anna. Thorfinnr told you to fight, and not run. I may not have been in your service when you were a child, but, if that tale he said to you before he left has any merit, and it did, because it got you out of bed, then I suggest for once, you fight." She stood from where she was kneeling beside the tub, "Whatever was just said to you by his Imperial Majesty…don't tell me. Just get up and do something about it." She tossed a strigil down into the water so it would splash up at her mistress.

Anna shrieked as her servant did this, but Samira was already out of the room by the time she managed to get to her feet.

--

The front was cold. Temperatures had dropped significantly overnight and the field of battle was covered by a fog which was slowly receding back to the Euxine Sea as the light grew. It was quiet. Too quiet.

Ragnvaldr and the rest of the Varangians were dressed in their bronze lamellar and tall helmets, axes in hand, as they marched with the other units. Ragnvaldr felt unsteady. This was the real thing. Not a drill, not a practice, the real thing. All he knew to do was essentially stick the other person with the sharp end of the ax. Simple enough, in theory. Sure, he had fought before, but now he was a farmer by trade, not a soldier. Skirmishes and drills do not a warrior make.

A trumpeter sounded his horn from further up the lines, and suddenly cries were heard from line commanders. There was already engagement. Ragnvaldr felt his stomach turn into a full knot.

Lines shored up and shields were raised. No numbers were known yet. No tactics or moving flanks, just fog and the sounds of clashing battle yards ahead. It could be minutes until they were called to the front, hours, or maybe days. It was hard to say.

"Axes!" Ragnvaldr shouted, and over one hundred guardsmen raised their long weapon into position. A few lines away, he could hear a line of men singing a liturgical hymn in Greek. Christian or not, he found it comforting. Faith is a powerful ally, no matter what faith it is.

"For Odin!" He shouted again, and the crowd cheered.

"For the endless food and drink of *Valhalla*!" Another cheer.

"For *Miklagaard!*" More cheering.

A different horn blew this time, along with it came a cry of, "*Varangoi!*"

It was time.

--

The horns and choir of the Hagia Sophia were loud and resonating within the dome of the basilica, making it hard to hear anything but the music.

The main doors opened and up the congregation turned to look as Anna walked in, veiled in red and gold and surrounded by attendants. Her *pallium* was heavily decorated with jewels and embroidery, and it trailed behind her a good ten feet.

The Emperor stood from his seat, while at the front, awaited the Patriarch of Constantinople. The choir continued to sing as Anna approached the head of the basilica, it seemed deafening and agonizing as the sung, poetic words of gospel and psalm resonated through her ears and mind.

Her head felt heavy with the jewels and pearls woven into her hair, and she wanted to jolt her head back, and gaze upon the great Christ *Pantokrator* looking down from the dome for a sign of salvation, of grace and calm in this hour, but she dare not stray her path even an inch. She reached the altar, and the red veil was stripped from her face to reveal her to the French duke awaiting her hand.

--

Ragnvaldr felt the blade of his ax cut into flesh for the first time. Startled, yet suddenly very invigorated, he watched the Bulgarian fall to the ground in front of him, his right shoulder separated at the joint where the trauma of the ax split the bone. The shards punctured the skin where it wasn't remaining attached to its owner by a strip of flesh that all but stopped the ax from completing its fall into the lungs completely on the side of his torso. It felt like ages as he watched the soldier cough and vomit blood as he reached to his killer with his violently shaking, intact arm, eyes wide, before collapsing in death.

So this is what it was like, and he had no time to either relish or be horrified at his act against humanity. He turned quickly to meet another opposing soldier, and blade met blade in a fury as more blood was spilled in this morning.

The Varangians hit the opposition's line with a sickening fury, one that the Bulgarians had not seen yet or were prepared to fully defend. The Imperial armies already outnumbered the Bulgarians at this point by a staggering ratio, but with adding the additional Northern men, the border skirmish became the equivalent of the Slavs running into an impenetrable stone wall.

With enough force, the axe cut through the steel of a Bulgarian's helmet as Ragnvaldr came down with a crushing blow against the side of his opponent's skull. The scratching sound it made against metal and then bone was sickening, but Ragnvaldr didn't stop, he couldn't. Something continued to drive him on. Another opponent: This time the ax came around into the Bulgarian's abdomen, slicing through his ineffective cuirass and right into his stomach, emptying his breakfast and bowels onto the wet steel.

As the sun had now completely risen over the field of battle, birds circled overhead, large and black. Ravens. The symbol of Odin himself was gracing the Varangians as they continued their slaughter into victory. It was so loud, deafeningly so, with the grinding of steel against steel and flesh, and the sounds of men crying out, in both victory and agony.

--

Anna was handed a candle to hold in her left hand, and she looked blankly at the tiled floor at the Patriarch's feet instead of the man she was being ritually betrothed to. The pearls on her headpiece felt cool against her face and neck, but they stiffened her, rather than relaxed, and the sweat in her hand around the large candle began to build.

The choir continued their chanting, even as the Patriarch began blessing the betrothal rings in front of the couple. Taking a ring in his hand, the Patriarch closed his fingers around it to form a fist, which he then raised to the Duke's forehead and made the sign of the cross while praying, and repeated this three times. After placing that ring onto the Duke's hand, he took the other ring, and moved toward Anna.

As he approached, she suddenly snapped out of her daze.

“No.”

The sound of the choir continued to drown her out, and he raised his hand to bless her.

“No!” She shouted and pulled away, nearly tripping over her *pallium* in the process.

The Emperor stood in his throne, and pointed toward her as she continued to protest.

“Seize her!”

Guardsmen moved toward Anna, and she darted away from them, dropping the candle which, extinguished itself as it shattered on the hard floor. The weight of her jeweled dress proved to be too much and, within moments, they had her in their arms.

--

"No!" Ragnvaldr cried out as he watched a section of his line suddenly disappear down the side of a drop. They fell hard into a river that was rapidly coursing into the sea, if the rocks didn't break their fall, first. The tables had turned, and the Bulgarians were advancing with a hard push.

The terrain was more dangerous than expected, and both sides struggled to maintain footing lest they plunge into the water next. With one off-thrust, Ragnvaldr lost control of his ax, and it sailed from his hand and down the ravine.

He reached behind his back, and was able to draw his scramasax from a sheath there. He dragged it under the armor of a Bulgarian's belly as he charged into him. Feeling the warm blood and entrails his hand at such a close range, Ragnvaldr felt himself grow sick. Within moments, his sight went black.

--

It took four Imperial guardsmen to finally get Anna under control, though she continued to struggle as much as she could before giving into exhaustion. The choir finally stopped chanting they realized she was restrained, and the basilica plunged into silence.

The Emperor stepped forward, and forcibly raised Anna's face to look upon him.

"You have disobeyed me for the last time." He sneered, forcibly squeezing her cheeks until she could taste blood on her tongue. “I recall giving you a choice of two options, not three. So either you look upon me now and choose the other, or you simply meet your fate.”

Anna remained silent, and forced saliva out of her mouth so that it would touch the Emperor’s hand.

Practically throwing her head aside when he let her go, he looked upon his guards and ordered, “Take her back to her chambers. There, she is to remain with little to no assistance. Put seven Varangians there. She is never to leave those walls until we pull her starved, dead body out from within them.

--

Ragnvaldr found himself sitting alone by the fire that evening, trying to recall exactly what had happened. He lost himself somewhere in battle, even though he was still very much alive and seemingly untouched, the pungent smell of dried blood and flesh on his clothing and armor almost made him feel intoxicated. The other men that survived today's encounter were also all back at camp, roasting food over their fires or assisting with the wounded, but the sounds of mixed languages and the vision of others surrounding Ragnvaldr just came off as a blur to him in his blood-drunk exhaustion.

He was snapped out of his haze when another Varangian walked by him, and threw a dirtied ax at his side.

“Fastger's.” The man said, “You lost yours, and he won't need it anymore.”

Ragnvaldr reached for the handle of the long ax, and looked it over. It reminded him a bit of his tools back home, and that he should be harvesting berries right now, not here, in Bulgaria, getting paid to fight for a country he had no allegiance to.

The stains of red that bled through onto his bleached linen smock only reminded him of the princess's veil. The lady whom, as far as he knew right now, was probably put to her death for saying another foul word to the disgusting Emperor of the service he was in. This whole adventure he was on seemed like nothing more than a joke now. A cruel, dark joke from Loki himself, making him feel miserable and alone.

--

"My lady!" Samira cried as she was dragged from the apartments with her children, "Please! Mercy!"

The Persian woman's husband lay dead on the floor in front of the main doors to Anna's apartments, but even as the princess tried to push through the guards in protest to save her servants, it was too late, and Samira was struck down by an Imperial guard to get her to quiet.

The children screamed in terror watching their mother fall in addition to their father, and Anna fell to her knees in disbelief with what was happening.

"Stop this!" She shouted, "Please in the name of Christ, stop this! They are innocent and good working people!"

"Quiet!" One of the guards kicked a boot against her, which only made Anna angry, and she got right back to her feet.

"How DARE you touch me!" She pushed herself into his face, "I am a member of the Imperial family and you will treat me as such and not a stray dog! Or I will have your head!"

"Not if the Emperor has your head first, Princess." The guard pushed her away.

This resulted in Anna striking the guard across the face with the back of her hand, much as she did Ragnvaldr only days earlier, but instead of standing down, the guard pinned her against the wall forcefully, and put his blade against her throat.

"Are you going to behave now, woman?" He sneered, blood dripping from his cheek from her rings, "Or will I have to take this one step further?"

"If you kill me, his Imperial Majesty will..."

"I never said anything about killing you." The guard interrupted, "Just taking a souvenir or two from your flesh."

Anna spat in his face, and the guard roared, and pushed against her harder, which caused her to scream. Another guard stepped in and covered her mouth, but she bit his hand hard, and he pulled back with a yelp of his own.

"Help!" She cried out, but the blade was against her neck again, this time actually pressing into her skin, and she could feel the searing hot pain of the blade slowly slicing into her.

"Shut up!" The guard yelled directly in her face.

Anna closed her eyes and held her breath. Then, the pressure of the blade and the guard's body against her was suddenly gone, and she opened her eyes to see Haakon ripping the man away from her with the crook of his ax.

"Now!" He yelled.

Anna pulled the sword that Thorfinnr had given her out from beneath her *pallium*, and thrust it into the other guard's ribs aiming beneath the arm that he was holding her with. He went down almost immediately, suffocating and coughing blood from his punctured lung as Anna withdrew her blade and ran for Samira's side.

The other Varangians were in the apartments now, and the Imperial guards that were attempting to secure Anna now had little chance.

"What is this treachery?" One of the guards yelled as he was surrounded by the ax-wielding Norsemen.

"We are here to protect the Emperor and the Imperial Family at all cost." Haakon replied, curtly.

"She's a prisoner!"

"She's an Imperial." Haakon raised his ax, "At all cost."

Anna closed her eyes as she heard the guard scream when the killing blow came down, but her attention was on Samira now, and her two, crying young daughters nearby.

"My lady..." Samira whispered out, "I'm sorry."

"Shh..." Anna put a hand on her beloved servant's face, "You have no reason to be sorry. I'm going to get you and your girls free of here."

"My husband...he is dead."

"I know..."Anna could feel her eyes burn as she tried to hold back tears as she watched Samira's own pool of blood spread around her.

"My children..." Samira stammered out, "Care for

them?"

"They will be safe. You have my word." Anna wiped her eyes, but her voice wavered.

Samira could speak no more, and it was evident by the harshness of her breath that it was her last. The older of the two girls was hugging her younger sister tightly as they both cried and prayed in the Persian language for the loss of their parents. Anna staggered up from where she was kneeling, and nearly lost her balance entirely before being caught by one of the Varangians.

"I have shed enough tears." She said to herself, before turning to the Norsemen, "Can we arrange for the girls to be brought to the barracks?"

"They can stay with some of the wives." Haakon replied, "There they will be safe." He motioned for one of the men to go over and aid the children, but they still seemed horrified by the loss of their parents. He didn't hesitate, however, and picked them both up before leaving the chambers with them howling the entire way out.

Anna watched in disgust as several of the Varangians were picking up the dead Imperial guards, and bringing their bodies to a window for them to be dumped into the sea. The sight of so much death in her foyer made her sick, and she began to heave a bit, but it emitted nothing.

"Pray attend the princess!" One of the guards called out, and a couple of the Varangians approached her to check on her well-being.

"I need to get out of here..." She said quietly.

"We cannot let you leave." Haakon replied, "I'm sorry...You know this. But we will keep you safe, and get you food so you are not starved."

Anna sighed, and went to retrieve the sword that Thorfinnr had given her, and, removing one of the silk veils still pinned onto her head, cleaned the blood from the blade.

"Princess..." Haakon approached her, "I promise you, as soon as we can find a way, you will be taken from Constantinople, forever."

CHAPTER 7
TRIALS

Back at the foggy Bulgarian Front, the battle was closing in on its first week. A messenger galloped with his horse around the various encampments and made his way up to the field of battle where the commanders were having their meeting.

"News from Constantinople!" he shouted, "I call for the Grand Domestic! News from Constantinople!"

Maxentios left the circle of men to approach the man as he dismounted his horse. The messenger reached into a saddle bag and pulled from it several pieces of rolled paper and handed them to the Grand Domestic, who, without so much as a word, returned to the commanders.

Opening the first scroll, he tossed it aside pretty quickly with a roll of his eyes, "New laws..." Then another one, "New taxes..." but the last one he got stuck on for a bit. His eyebrows raised, and he forced his breath out of pursed lips as he narrowed his gaze toward the paper.

"My brother's wife," He began, and looked right at Ragnvaldr, "The Lady Anna Dokeianina Syrakousina, defied the Emperor by deliberately causing a scene during her betrothal ceremony to Duke...whatever, I can't read French names. She's being detained by the Varangians in her quarters until her sentence is carried out."

Ragnvaldr remained silent, and his eyes fell to the ground.

"Either exile," Maxentios smirked, "Or, death. Dear me, what has my darling sister gotten herself into this time? Always has been the one to get herself in trouble. Ever since they brought her to the city as a girl, she's been nothing but a feisty little nuisance. Silly islanders, especially since she's half barbarian anyway...Well, perhaps a bit more than half, now." his eyes moved back to Ragnvaldr, "Would you care to read it?"

"No, sir." He replied, solemnly.

"Good, it appears you have your own." Maxentios handed him one of the letters, and Ragnvaldr reluctantly took it.

As Ragnvaldr unfolded the paper, he saw that the letter was in the Norse language, but the name of the sender was the most important. It was from Anna, but written in Haakon's hand. Only skimming it briefly, and still barely paying any attention to it, he snorted, and tossed it in the fire.

“Must not have been important.” Maxentios chided.

“No.” Ragnvaldr replied softly, and walked away silently from the commander's meeting.

--

“Do you think he got it?” Anna paced in her room, “Do you think that they would confiscate letters?”

“I did what I could to make sure that it made it to the messenger.” Haakon replied from where he was standing guard with the other Varangians by her doors.

“I still don't understand this all...” She shook her head, “I'm still so confused.”

“*Kyria,*” Haakon spoke, “If I may speak freely, I suggest you get some rest. Perhaps then your mind will find peace. If what you told me of the Emperor is true, your life is in grave danger. Now is not the time to dwell on…”

“…His mind changed so quickly.” Anna continued, despite his interruption, “He was so abrupt to just...leave me at the first sign of threat.”

“Anna...” Haakon spoke more informally to get her attention, “Anna...you must know. Ragnvaldr’s wife is with child.”

She stopped in her tracks, and turned back to the Varangian at the door, whom she had trusted for many years, and gave him a glare that plainly stated she was far above him in status, and he needed to speak cautiously.

“You speak treasonous words to me.”

Haakon shook his head, “No, my Princess. I wish I could say that his affections were only yours, but I fear that you have been cheated.”

“Where is this woman? Is she in the barracks?”

“Yes, your Highness.”

“Cut the formalities...can you bring her here?”

“I can arrange it if my lady desires it.”

“I do. See to it that this wife of Ragnvaldr's is brought to me.” Anna found a chair near a window and sat down, biting her fist in anger. “I wish to have words with her.”

--

“You never told her?” One of the Varangians sitting at the fire next to Ragnvaldr said to him. “If she ever found out, she could very easily have your wife's head.”

“It was a mistake,” Ragnvaldr shook his head, “that's all.”

“I don't believe you.” The other guard snorted, “You've been looking for a way out for some time. I just never bet on it being with an Imperial.”

“Doesn't matter now.” Ragnvaldr replied, “She's probably dead now, anyway.”

“Who, your wife?”

“No. One could hope.” Ragnvaldr poked at the fire

with a stick, "Anna."

--

"Your Imperial Highness," A couple of Varangians walked in with a startled looking woman with them, "Allow us to present to you the wife of Ragnvaldr Gunnarsson."

Anna looked at the other woman with a face of pure disgust, which could not be concealed. She wasn't anything remarkable, in the least. Much like how Ragnvaldr described the women of the North being just as the men, with coarse skin, she could now see this for herself. Women living in the barracks with the Varangians were not often allowed out. They were essentially camp followers, and kept there to help keep house, and satisfy the men, but she did know that many guards were married and had their spouses with them. Ragnvaldr managed to withhold this information.

His wife was not at all what Anna was expecting. Dark in hair and complexion, this meant that she was probably from a more Eastern land. Her dress was of a course wool and linen, affixed with large bronze brooches at the shoulders, and bulging over her swollen belly. Her face was long and plain, almost horse-like, and her black eyes pierced right into Anna, who recognized her immediately.

"You." She stated, "You attacked us on the street!"

The woman said nothing, and stared at Anna with black eyes filled with anger and hatred.

"Can you understand me?" Anna said in Norse.

The woman went off on a tirade in her native tongue, which was a dialect that Anna wasn't familiar with except for a few words, and she moved toward Anna angrily before she was pulled back by the guards.

"What did she say?"

Haakon sighed, "Most of those words, I'm afraid, are not fit for the ears of an Imperial lady."

"Tell her I mean her no harm, I just wanted to see her with my own eyes. It's just unfortunately that we have seen each other before, and my generosity to her was careless on my part."

Haakon translated, and the woman, once again went off on a tirade, walked forward and spat at Anna in her anger. This resulted in the two guards holding her to grab her forcefully to subdue her.

"You disgusting barbarian." Anna sneered as she stepped away from the spit, "How dare you treat a member of the Imperial Household with such disrespect? You do not know me, or the circumstances in which I know your husband."

"She said that it was your fault he is gone." Haakon said, "And that he told her of you before he left for war. I must apologize, Princess, she is known for her erratic behavior."

"How did she get here?"

"Camp follower. Ragnvaldr impregnated her, and then she blew a fit until they were wed."

"Disgusting filthy whore." Anna hissed, and raised a hand to strike the woman, but refrained, and stepped away. "No. My quarrel is not with her." She looked at her former lover's wife, and felt her own pain mirrored in the woman's eyes. "Get her out of here. She doesn't deserve to see the interior of the palaces, or know the life I could have given her husband were he honest with me. Don't tell her that. Just tell her…I'm sorry. I know how she feels."

As the guards pulled the Norse woman from the apartments, she turned, and, with a menacing grin, said to Anna in Greek, "Disgusting...filthy...whore."

Anna felt her skin grow hot and her hands shake as the woman was pulled from her rooms, laughing to herself, and waited until the doors were closed tight between them before she turned to Haakon.

"I'm sorry." He said to her softly.

She raised a hand to silence his words, and motioned for him to follow her.

"I will write again to the fronts." She hurried to a desk in her parlor, "And, I will also write to my son in Bulgaria..."

--

"*Ragnvaldr,*

I write you this letter in hopes of a reply. Your sudden departure left me empty, and I only wish that you would be honorable. Terrible events have happened since you left. You need to pay attention to these words…"

Ragnvaldr bit his lip as he read the second letter than was brought from Constantinople in the week, emitted a sigh, and began to rip it up.

"Huh." He went, walking toward the fire.

"What is it?" A nearby Varangian asked, "Another letter of affection from the princess? Is she all right?"

Ragnvaldr shook his head, "I just wish she would leave me alone." And threw the letter into the fire. "I...I need to be. I want to be alone."

--

Anna sat in silence in her parlor, and sighed.

"I'm sorry, Princess." Haakon leaned on his ax and looked down at her. "I wish there was something I could tell you. Something that would make you feel better. Something, perhaps, that would brighten your day, but I know that words are simply that."

"I should have never come back to the capital." She replied.

"Why did you not take the marriage to the Frenchman?" Haakon asked, "He would have provided for you for the rest of your days, and you would have been able to leave."

Anna just shook her head, "It was wrong. The

Emperor was setting me up for destruction by other means. I directly disobeyed him, yes, but, there, in Hagia Sophia, I felt a divine presence tell me to not go forward."

"It is your northern spirit."

"I am not from the North." Anna's eyes were gazing out the window by this point, watching the waves lightly lap against the seawall below.

"Sometimes, "Haakon began, "Spoken word is unnecessary. You may be a Greek woman, born on the waters of the South, educated in ways that I have never been, but you are driven to the North. It calls to you. Its very snows are reflected in your eyes. You may not be of the North, my lady, but it is very much a part of you."

The doors to the main chamber opened, and an Imperial guard-flanked herald entered without as much as a knock.

They had Anna surrounded at her seat in no time, and the Varangians, although holding their axes in defense, were told to stand down.

"Your Highness." The herald began, "His Imperial Majesty orders that you appear before him in court to accept the charges places against you as a traitor to the Empire, and to be given your sentence."

Anna felt her heart leap into her chest.

"My sentence." She said softly, and stood from her chair. The Imperial guards surrounded her, and immediately moved to take her arms.

"I go in peace." She raised her hands and avoided their touch, looked back at Haakon, and took a deep breath. "Lead the way, herald."

The entourage walked somberly to the main hall of the Great Palace complex, where, just months prior, Anna returned to Constantinople. Where she knelt before the new Emperor, and saw Ragnvaldr for the first time. Where she had defied the Emperor in front of the pilgrims, and once sat as a member of the Imperial household. Now, Anna was entering the hall for what was probably the last time, to plead for her life and meet her fate.

Marble was a cold and unforgiving arena for the sport of law, but Anna entered without a struggle, and stood there in the eyes of so many she once called family and peers to meet her judgment.

"Anna Dokeianina, *Kyria* Syrakousina, *Prinkípissa* Komnene." The herald began, "You are hereby brought before the court of his Imperial Majesty to atone for your crimes of treason by deliberately going against his words, which is the word of the Lord, and of the state. How do you confess?"

Anna's throat felt scratchy, and she could feel sweat oozing from every pore of her body.

"I confess that I deliberately disobeyed his Majesty." Anna began softly, "I was thinking only of my..."

"That will be enough, *Kyria* Syrakousina." The herald interrupted, and motioned for the Emperor to speak.

The Emperor sat in his chair, looking way too satisfied at himself for these proceedings, and cracked a smile before he began to speak, "Anna..." He sighed, "Anna, Anna...What am I to do with you?" He stood from his throne, put his hands behind his back, and walked down from the dais to where the lady stood.

"What am I to do with a woman, who disobeys me with such...fire? And grace? A woman whom I call cousin, even if only by marriage? What do I do with a traitor, Anna? Tell me?"

"You execute them, My Emperor."

"I execute them!" He shouted to the rest of the court, "Very good, Anna. I execute them, and usually with little time to think otherwise. However, you are a member of the Imperial household, and as such, I can't kill you as easily without the odds of some dirty Slav or Norman army appearing at my walls. No. You arranged that marriage with your son for a reason didn't you? You want there to be war."

"I would never put my son or the Empire in danger!"

"Silence!" The Emperor commanded, and put a hand to her face, "In addition to that, we have caught your precious letters to the front, and copied them. I have also received word from the Grand Domestic of yet even more treachery. In love with a heathen barbarian, are you? May your husband turn in his grave! You must have more of your mother in you than I thought."

The court erupted in chatter, and Anna suddenly felt

naked, and betrayed. Suddenly, death seemed like a keener option than exile. It would free her from life, a life she detested and never belonged in. She would be at total peace.

"I wear my barbarism honorably." She raised her head, "My mother, the Varangians. No, we may not bleed purple, My Emperor, but we bleed red, the red of the Dokeianos. Red, just as you do."

"You wish to see my blood flow, then?"

"I wish to see this great empire restored to what it was." Anna began, "And I wish nothing more for myself, and the ones I love, to be at peace, finally."

"You speak as if your life here is torment." The Emperor glared at her.

"For the seventeen years I have spent living in Constantinople, my Emperor, "Anna began, "I was without torment for many periods, and all were before you stole the throne."

The court erupted again, and Anna stood there, perfectly still, in her petals of red silk, staring right back at the man who had the power to end her life.

"Enough!" the Emperor commanded, "At this point, Dokeianina, you have one option, and that is the chance to plead for your life."

"In either exile or death, my Emperor, you release me from Constantinople, and your control." Anna stood her ground, "I will be free of you, and this prison you call the palace. Free of the court, and free of the Church. A more fitting punishment would be to keep me alive and in my cell here in the palace for eternity."

"Shut up." the Emperor turned, and raised a hand to strike Anna, but she didn't even so much as flinch, and seeing this, he lowered his hand, and turned his back to her one final time.

"Kill her."

Anna lowered her eyes to the floor, and felt every muscle in her body give up with the announcement of her sentence. Imperial guards took her arms forcefully, and she looked up for a moment to see the faces of the Varangians behind the throne. Their eyes gave away their stone-faced expressions. Her friends, the only men in the entire capital that Anna had ever been able to trust, were now powerless due to the oath they swore when they arrived in Constantinople to serve the Emperor. She was abandoned, her secrets naked to the court, and soon, her head would be added to the growing Imperial collection.

"Write to my son." She said softly, "Tell him. Tell him everything."

The Emperor turned back to face Anna, a grin slowly spreading on his face. "My dear cousin, have you wondered why your son has not returned your letters since he left for his marriage?"

The pain that Anna felt, at this precise moment, was greater than anything she had ever imagined, and she knew that what she was about to hear, was probably worse than any torturous death the maniacal man in front of her could ever give her.

"No..." She started shaking her head, "No...No..." Her words were stuck, and she started to feel her legs completely give below her.

"Reports have it," The Emperor's lips were nearly arching to his ears, "That he cried out for you until he was finally silenced by the Varangian's ax that killed him."

The internal pain ripped Anna in half from her toes to her eyes. She lost her ability to stand immediately and fell to the marble floor in a shaking heap held up by the guards grasping her arms.

"Perhaps it was Ragnvaldr that killed him?" The Emperor's pride in his own actions was like a twisting knife in Anna's side, "That would have been grand, indeed!"

Anna was without words, and could only watch as the tears from her eyes formed a small puddle on the floor below her.

The Emperor knelt on the floor to try to get a view of the pain on the woman's face, and grinned.

"Where is that strength you had before to stand, Anna?" He said to her coldly, "Before you were so sure to ask for your death, and yet, you now know, you truly have nothing left to live for."

The Empress stood up, then. Her own eyes reddened with emotion, "Stop this madness!" She shouted, "How could you?"

"Be quiet, girl!" The Emperor shouted at her, "I would have killed her father too, had reports not come back of that Norman lord and his crew, sailing into Sicily with that barbarian, Thorfinnr, and removing Dokeianos from the island to safety! The family will no longer be in my way of controlling my Rome once Anna is executed!"

Anna's eyes widened as she heard that her father had been taken by the pilgrims sailing to Andalusia, but she continued to stare at the floor.

"I never wanted Rome." She whispered, barely able to speak, "But she doesn't belong to you…"

"Release her!" The young Empress commanded, "She has done nothing of treason! And you are mad!"

The Emperor pointed at his wife, "Remove her from my court! I will deal with her later." He turned back to Anna, "Get her to the prisons. Strip her of her wealth, and prepare the ax man's stand for tomorrow. We will make a spectacle of what happens when even Imperials become treacherous." Turning back to the Empress, he narrowed his eyes, "Maybe even two."

Anna gave no resistance to the guards walking her to her cell, or as they looted her person for jewels. The pain had turned to numbness, and, when the iron bars closed behind her, all she could do was sink to the cold, dirt floor slowly. Her chest felt truly hollow, and her heartbeat seemed to echo in the silence of the prison. Sitting in solitude until nightfall, was the woman who was once a lady of the courts of Constantinople now wished for dawn and her death to come more swiftly.

When darkness had fallen and taken over for a few hours, Haakon appeared at her cell, along with two other men that Anna recognized as Halfdan and Wulfhere, and startled her suddenly.

They immediately motioned for her to stay quiet as they unlatched her door, and motioned for her to come to them.

Anna sat there, wide eyed, at this sudden shift of luck. "I have nothing more to live for, my friends." She whispered to them, "Leave me in peace."

"I think not." Haakon reached in and took her arm to pull her to her feet. "Either you die here, or you die trying to escape. Us men from the North, my lady, we fight to the end, and I assure you, this is not over for you, yet."

He handed her a bundle of clothes, "Put these on, and cut your braids. We ride past the walls tonight."

Anna was grabbed by her arms to stand, and was handed a knife by one of the men. With a wince, took them against the base of her braided hair, and let the woven strands fall to the floor where she was once laying. As soon as Anna was changed into the tunic and trousers of a Norseman, the men escorted her out as fast and quietly as they could, past the several dead prison guards who lay in pools of their own blood.

They ushered her into the barracks, where they had bags and purses of her effects waiting for her, along with the sword that Thorfinnr had given her.

“I can't believe you're doing this.” She said, as they wrapped her in a cloak and put a wool cap on her head. “You will die if they catch us.”

Haakon just smiled, “At all cost, Princess. At all cost.”

Horses were loaded with their belongings and supplies, and Anna was placed on a cart to be pulled, full of various weapons and food stuffs, destined for the men in Bulgaria.

“We ride to the front?” She asked.

“No.” Haakon replied, “We ride to the West, to Italy. I've dispatched a man to the front, bringing news to Ragnvaldr and the other men of the happenings. We need to get you as far away from the Empire as possible. In Italy we will get you on a ship to Andalusia. You will be safe there with your father and the pilgrims Thorfinnr traveled with.

“What are the odds of us actually being able to get out of the boundaries of the empire without being caught?” Anna seemed hesitant.

“We’ll find out as soon as we try.” Haakon answered.

“We're going to have company very soon if we don't leave immediately.” Halfdan stepped up to the cart, and handed Anna her blade. “You keep that at the ready, whatever you do. It's going to be a bumpy ride out.”

By the time they arrived at the *Xylokerkos* Gate, the alarm was raised that the prisoner had escaped, and security at the walls had tripled. Anna pulled the cap as low over her head as she could, and sat in the back of the cart as Haakon and Wulfhere were stopped by guards and interrogated by the guards.

"Just goods to the front." Haakon said, deliberately speaking Greek with a heavy accent, "And the boy, a page to the commanders."

A guard rounded to the cart, and Anna sat there, trembling, but trying not to do so visibly.

"You! Barbarian!" The guard asked, "State your name."

Anna deepened her voice, and immediately started speaking Norse, but mostly gibberish.

The guard just shook his head and said, "Shut up, heathen! You are clear to pass. Get on with you."

As they passed through the gate, Anna watched from the back of the cart as the striped walls of Theodosius grew distant until she could no longer see them. The city of Constantinople was at last, behind her.

CHAPTER 8
AT ALL COST

The Varangian messenger rode into Bulgaria at breakneck speeds, and quickly found his way to the encampment of his brethren. Jumping down from his horse, he ran toward the blood-covered, bronze-armored Norsemen returning from another day at battle.

"Ragnvaldr!" He ran up to the acting commander, and threw his hands on his shoulders, looking him straight in the eyes, "They're going to kill her."

Ragnvaldr blinked a few times, and shook off the messenger to walk around him.

"Haakon sent me, listen!" the messenger was relentless, and stayed at Ragnvaldr's heels until he was acknowledged. "Anna is to be put to death for treason, but Haakon was aiming to free her. If he did, they were headed west to get her to Thorfinnr. Ragnvaldr, listen!"

He forcefully turned the bloodied commander around to face him, "They killed her son...Her own son, Ragnvaldr! The young prince who was to stop this war! Don't you see? The Emperor, he is seeing us all to death!

He means to eliminate anyone that stands in his way. We're just being used, and now the princess could be in her grave! Don't stand for this; you need to see to her!"

"I can't." Ragnvaldr replied, emotion in his voice as he turned from the messenger, "I have a line to command. A duty and an oath to uphold, and...A family to provide for. I can't chase after a runaway princess in attempts to save her life while I fight for my own. I'm sorry."

The messenger just shook his head, "Then I was wrong thinking you were a better man."

Ragnvaldr had started to walk away, but stopped with those words.

"That woman with your child," the messenger began, "If it is even your child, is no lady. She is a mad creature looking for easy handouts. You, like the rest of us, took a vow to protect the Emperor and his family. To the hells with the Emperor, Ragnvaldr! Love or no, Anna needs you. Now more than ever. Find her, and bring her to safety. Be the strong, heroic warrior you always spoke of being."

Ragnvaldr pulled the pendant given to him by Anna from beneath his tunic and armor, and gazed at it while the messenger spoke.

"Now is your chance to make yourself a saga."

Ragnvaldr gripped the medallion tightly, and closed his eyes as he felt the cool metal against his warm palm.

"Show me the way to the road to the West." He said softly, "I'll leave under cover of darkness."

--

Anna washed her face with water from the river they had stopped alongside to rest. She filled a bowl with some, and threw in a splash of wine to make it drinkable before swallowing the contents rapidly. She laid back on the riverbank, reaching for her hair that was no longer there, and starred up at the clear, blue sky of the next day.

"How far away are we?" She asked.

"Maybe twenty miles." Haakon replied. "We can probably push for another thirty by dark. We can't risk the horses."

"It just doesn't seem far enough when there are hundreds to be covered."

"We will get you there, my lady. I promise you."

--

Ragnvaldr was on the road in pursuit of Anna within minutes after true darkness overcame Bulgaria, and followed the messenger partway until the roads split between Constantinople and the Western lands.

Desertion of the army was a serious offense, and he knew that his freedom would be very short lived unless he made it as far as the others were, and even then, it would not be a guarantee. He would be pursued, and so would she, and this Emperor would stop at nothing to see them both dead. He knew there was a detachment coming. He couldn't see or hear them, but he could feel it. It would take them a week to get past the borders of the Empire, at least, and the terrain would grow difficult as they would pass through Greece toward Latin lands. But they had to push, they had to try.

Now he could hear them behind him. A hundred horses to his one, who was in bad need of a break. He slowed and allowed his horse to veer into the woods and slow his path, but he knew he couldn't let them pass him. That would be her inevitable death that would ride by if he did.

Ragnvaldr led his horse down a hill toward a riverside where it could drink, and noticed something on the bank nearby, shining through the pebbles. He reached down to retrieve the object, and found it to be a silver ring that he was all too familiar with, as his face bore a scar along the cheek where it ripped into his flesh. It was one of Anna's many pieces of jewelry, probably dropped from a purse. He then saw foot and hoof prints, and ran to follow them until they disappeared where they were deliberately swept away by tree branches.

He couldn't determine which way from that point that they returned to the road, or even if they crossed the river, but what he did know is that she was still alive, and not far ahead.

"They were here." He said out loud, placing the ring in a pouch on his belt.

"And so are we." The Grand Domestic answered, standing directly behind Ragnvaldr, and dealing him a blow when he turned around that rendered him unconscious. His body was tossed across the back of a commander's horse, and brought back to Constantinople within a day's ride.

The next thing Ragnvaldr knew, he woke up to feeling extremely warm, and dizzy, and knew he was fighting off an infection. His head throbbed where he was struck and he could feel the tightness from the scabbing and dried blood in the area.

Groaning, he rolled in place where he was laying, and fell hard onto a dirt and straw floor. Spitting some of it from his mouth, he pulled himself into a sitting position and put his head in his hands, trying to control his nausea as the taste of acid and bile rose in his throat. He felt himself gag, and then relaxed before checking his hand to see the extent of the blood cake on his temple.

He heard a woman's laughter from outside of his cell, and turned his head to see his wife there, sitting on the floor outside of the bars, her tummy bulging, and giving him a psychotic smile before laughing again at his predicament.

"Fool." She hissed. "Disgusting dog, you are."

"Woman, silence." He commanded, but she just started laughing again, and beckoned him to the bars.

"You want out?" She asked.

"If it means having to deal with you all the time? No."

More laughter and the horse-faced woman clutched her belly, "You make me laugh, dog. Now come, I free you."

"Bail." She replied, and held up the necklace that Anna had given Ragnvaldr, and laughed again, "Enough gold, yes? Very pretty, mmm, shiny and pretty. Like a dead princess."

"You bitch." Ragnvaldr moved toward the bars, "How did you get that? That is not yours. Give it back!"

"Freedom?" His wife asked, "No? Still, very pretty." She put the necklace on and posed with it on, "Princess, right?"

Ragnvaldr shook his head and grumbled in Greek, "You'll never be a princess; you don't deserve to wear that. Ever."

"Disgusting whore." His wife replied in the only Greek words she knew, "Disgusting whore!"

"I wonder how you learned that phrase." Ragnvaldr growled as he curled into a ball, and put his aching head onto his crossed arms where they clutched his knees.

She started laughing again and took off the necklace before using the bars to help her to her feet. "I'll get guard." She said to him, "You stay, dog, stay!"

His wife whistled, and waved the necklace in the direction of the prison guard, who approached, and looked it over.

"Please don't take it." Ragnvaldr asked the man in Greek, "It's not hers to give. My life is not worth that."

But the guard didn't listen, and took the necklace from Ragnvaldr's wife before unlocking and unlatching the cell door, and allowing Ragnvaldr to have his freedom restored.

The pendant was tucked away on the guard's person in seconds, and the gift that Anna had given Ragnvaldr for saving her life, her family heirloom, was suddenly gone. A life debt repaid, indeed.

Ragnvaldr took to his feet slowly and walked from the cell, glaring at his wife the entire time.

"You miserable, jealous bitch." He said to her, "I wish I never met you. I wish you would have just left me to be."

His wife laughed again, and grabbed his arm as if in an

embrace.

"Come home, dog. I'll feed you." She said. "I'll make you better, again."

Ragnvaldr pulled his arm from her grasp, but she protested and started to flail after him. Without much effort, he pushed her aside, and walked out of the prison ahead of her.

"Dog!" His wife called after him. "You cannot save her."

Sighing, Ragnvaldr turned around to look at the crazy woman behind him, the one that he had allowed himself to be bound to, out of what was supposedly the right thing to do.

"What?" He asked, halfheartedly.

"You cannot save princess." She grinned, and then made a motion across her neck while making a gurgling sound in the back of her throat, "Dead. Dead yesterday."

Ragnvaldr watched his wife, and listened to her broken words. Although he had done his best to separate his emotions from Anna, he closed his eyes, and turned back to leaving as he heard the woman cackle behind his back as he exited into the fresh air back in Constantinople. Now he knew exactly what he meant when Anna told him that this city, in itself, was a prison. He could probably never escape now, just as she couldn't.

--

Anna found herself staring at the looming silhouette of the Balkan Mountains as they made their way into Thrace. The air was starting to grow colder as they went up in elevation, and she clutched the cloak around her body as the two Varangians and she overlooked their next obstacle.

"How are we going to make it through those?" She asked, "This is insanity, now I know why most travelers come by boat."

"There are roads, ancient ones." Haakon said, "They are maintained."

"And patrolled, no doubt." Anna grimaced, "Well, we've come this far. We need to pass them. Italy is on the other side."

Wulfhere said something, but as he was Saxon, Anna could not understand, and she looked to Haakon.

"What is it?" She asked.

Haakon merely walked toward the cart, and began unhitching it from the horses.

"What are you doing?" Anna asked, "Are you mad?"

Haakon remained silent for a bit more until he finished the process, and handed Anna her blade.

"My lady." He said softly, "They're coming. You need to run."

"What?" Anna starting shaking her head, "No...I can't cross these mountains without you. I can't get there. I don't know where to go."

Wulfhere said something again, and Haakon pointed, "That is the direction to the road that will take you safely through the mountains and to the Adriatic Sea. You are two weeks out. Take the black horse, as she is already laden with your belongings."

"You're serious." Anna backed up.

"They are coming for you, Anna. Look!" Haakon pointed in the distance, and sure enough, she could see motion from the hill they were on. It was the Grand Domestic's detachment, and they were heading straight for them.

"Can they see us?"

"Not yet, but they will, soon." Haakon led Anna to the horse, and made sure she could mount the saddle on her own. "This is why you need to go."

"What about you?" She asked. "You aren't..."

"Haakon looked grim, and Wulfhere loaded a pack of food and water onto the back of the horse just behind Anna.

"We're going to buy you time, but it won't be much." Haakon backed away from the horse, and went to retrieve a weapon from the cart.

Anna suddenly felt the pit of her stomach turn, and sat there on the horse, looking down at the two Varangians who had freed her.

"Anna, there are no time for goodbyes. Ride." Haakon backed away from the horse, "Ride! Girl! We will see you again in the afterlife if our gods will it! Go!"

Swallowing hard, she took one final glance back at the men, and then started off in a gallop toward the road, holding tightly to the reigns of the beast as she did, and holding back tears as she prayed aloud.

"Heavenly Father, protect those men who have done so much to see to my freedom. And see to it that their families are forever blessed with your mercy...WHOA!"

The prayer ended with a blockade of Imperial soldiers, spears in hand, waiting for her to come down the hill and onto the ancient Roman road.

"We have you now, Princess!" Their commander stepped forward as soon as her horse calmed down, "Perhaps you should finish your prayers."

The hilt of her sword shone from its scabbard at the side of the horse's frame. She couldn't take them all, as she was not that skilled, and they had projectile weapons, but she smiled anyway.

"Perhaps I will see you in the afterlife, my friends." She felt her eyes sting when her thoughts went to the two Varangians as she reached for the blade, "Because I was obviously praying to the wrong god!"

In one swift movement, she retrieved the sword and threw it directly at the commander, which caught him and his men completely off-guard as it caught his neck and slit his throat in a stroke of pure luck, and he fell to a gurgling, bleeding mess on the ground.

Immediately the men started to advance against her, and the horse reared back and turned back in the other direction, but it was too late, as it was perfectly clear that in the time it took her to get down the hill, that the detachment had it completely surrounded, and she met with another line of spearmen and her smiling brother-in-law in just a few gallops.

"Hold!" Maxentios shouted, "Do not attack her. It's been requested that she's brought back alive." He grinned even wider, "So she can go back to Constantinople."

Anna glared down at the Grand Domestic from the horse, and suddenly wished she had saved her blade.

"Damn you to the Hells." Anna sneered.

"Hells? Lucky me there is more than one. Oh, your precious Varangians!" Max danced a bit, "You must wonder how they fared. Here, let me give you a puppet show."

The heads of both Haakon and Wulfhere were raised on tall spears to the laughter of the men surrounding her, but for some reason, Anna remained unfazed.

"I'm going to die, Max." She smiled, "I've known this now for days, if not weeks. All you're proving now is my worth, and that the greatest Empire in the world is starting to lose its hold. If one woman can slip through the Emperor's hand so easily, how much more will he lose? He's lost Sicily, he's losing Bulgaria and Asia Minor, and soon he will lose everything."

"Get her off of the horse." Maxentios ordered, "Put her in the cart with the dead."

Anna slid off of the black stallion herself, and stood there, staring at her brother-in-law with a cold glare. "There's a place for you still in my heart, Max. In the darkest corner where the poison I kissed from your brother's lips has found a home. I pray that the same poison finds its place in your own."

--

"A messenger just came back into the court." Halfdan came back into the barracks in a hurry, "She's alive...they have her."

Ragnvaldr shot up out of his bunk, "What?"

"Alive! Anna is alive! The Grand Domestic caught up to her in Thrace. They're on their way back to the...where are you going? If they see you're free you will die!"

Ragnvaldr was suddenly armored, "I'm no longer waiting for my saga."

He ran out of the barracks in a shot, running toward the stables to grab the first available tacked horse. The sun was starting to set, and horns sounded in the distance from the walls. The army was approaching. It was now or never.

He rode straight out of the Great Palace complex, through the Hippodrome and out onto the first main street that would get him to a gate. The windows around Hagia Sophia's dome reflected the light of the sun as he rode past the massive basilica and toward the impenetrable, ancient walls of Constantinople for hopefully the last time, and he exited at the *Xylokerkos* Gate to see the army making their grand entrance with their captive on the *Via Egnatia* through the Golden Gate near the sea. The detachment marched in perfect parade formation, led by the Grand Domestic, as if they were heroes for managing to retrieve one woman from a hundred miles away.

Anna's hands were bound as she sat on the cart filled with rotting dead, and ornamented with the swollen, rotting heads of her martyred Varangians, but she stayed focused, and looked straight ahead as they pulled into the gate...that is until Ragnvaldr intercepted the cart, and ripped the rider from his horse with a short ax. This got the attention of the rest of the unit very quickly, even though the first half was already well through the gate and still parading in as conquerors.

Shocked out of her focus, Anna wasted no time jumping from the cart once it stopped completely and running for the embattlement of the lower wall while Ragnvaldr continued to create the diversion. Arrows rained from the sky from the guards in the towers of the wall, but Anna was able to slip into hiding easily as she once did in her childhood.

Ragnvaldr leapt from his horse, and ran in her direction, but the army was in hot pursuit. This made Anna thankful, as she was able to run while he was distracting the archers. She ran the length of the wall from the gate toward the seawall, concealed by the shadows of the taller walls, until she had Propontis in her sights by the Marble Tower. At this point, all soldiers had lost sight of her, and the firing in her direction stopped.

After cutting her hands free on a felled arrow, she climbed up onto the seawall, and then over the side where she could get her footing on a ledge. She scaled toward a niche, and held herself there for a while, waiting until the commotion above faded.

"She must have fallen into the sea!"

"She's not here!"

"Where did she go?"

"Did she fall into the sea?"

"She's gone!"

"She's dead! She fell into the sea!"

Anna heard the same sentences over and over again, and didn't relax her grip on the wall until the voices were well off in the distance. Closing her eyes, she took in a deep breath of the salted air, and laughed a bit to herself as she listened to the waves below. She was finally free.

She opened her eyes to see a single boat coming in off of the horizon, and smiled. Despite the chaos above, and despite everything that had just transpired in mere months after returning to Constantinople, she felt absolute peace, and allowed her eyes to burn with tears one more time.

"Anna..." A familiar, soft voice spoke, which almost made her lose her balance and fall into the water below.

"Anna!"

"...Ragnvaldr?"

"You're alive!"

"So...are you."

Ragnvaldr had seen Anna climb onto the seawall, and followed suit one he was free of the falling arrows. He scaled his way over to where Anna was in her niche, and looked at her, his mouth partially open in awe. She turned to face him, still supporting herself against the wall, but her expression was emotionless.

"Come on." He said, "Let's get out of here. Let's get you to freedom."

"I...am free."

"Anna...please."

"No." She shook her head and closed her eyes. "At this moment, I have seen everything, lost everything...there is nothing more, Ragnvaldr. I want you to go." She shook her head and moved a few bricks away from him carefully, if not gracefully.

"You've gone mad." He tried to bring himself closer to her, but his grip on the stone wasn't as strong as hers, and he hugged the wall's surface tightly.

She shook her head again. "You once chased me to

these walls on a different night. It seems so long ago now, that night I lost my heart to you."

"Anna...I'm sorry." He could feel his throat tighten, "If I could go back I...I would make everything right."

"Would you?" She asked, turning around so that her back was to the water and she could face him. "You betrayed me."

"I should never have acted the way that I did. I can only ask for your forgiveness."

Anna looked at him, her blue eyes wet with tears, and she forced a laugh, "I am here, right now, on this wall above the sea, penniless, dressed like a man, at the expense of the lives of men who have been in my service since I was a young mother, for taking a chance. A chance I thought I could have changed my life." She looked back out at the water, at the boat, which was now closer, and then back to him, "It did change my life. It cost me the life of my son. It cost me everything…where is that necklace I gave you?"

Ragnvaldr froze, not expecting her to notice so quickly, "It saved my life...just as you gave it to me for saving yours."

"Then my debt to you is paid." Anna said shortly, and turned back to the water, "Go, Ragnvaldr. Go to your family...Or better yet, go home, to the North and far away from here. Run...Run as you did from me, and from your problems just like Thorfinnr accused me of doing. Leave Constantinople, and never come back."

"My oath..." He contradicted, but couldn't finish.

"It means nothing, now." Anna interrupted, "Your head is marked, and you will be hunted to the ends of the earth if you do not leave now." She looked from the water below up to the height of the walls. "They're looking for you, can you swim?"

"No, I can't. What about you?"

"What about me?" She asked, "As far as they are concerned," She pointed upwards, "I'm already dead. As I said, I have nothing left to lose...You; you still haven't lost everything, yet."

"I know I still have a piece of your soul." Ragnvaldr's eyes were beginning to water, "What do you want me to do with it?"

"Keep it, or destroy it, perhaps, as it no longer functions as it once did." She said, and looked him straight in his blue eyes for one last time. "Goodbye."

And with those words, she released her hold on the seawall, took a deep breath, closed her eyes, and allowed herself to gently fall back into the depths of Propontis.

"NO!" Ragnvaldr yelled, "No..." He watched as her body plunged into the dark waters, and then disappeared as the foam from her splash dissolved.

"There!" A shout came from overhead, "I heard something! Look! The Varangian!"

Ragnvaldr snapped out of the shock of watching the woman appear to kill herself. Anna was right, they were still after him. He needed to run.

--

Maxentios made it to the palace quietly despite the continuing commotion. There, the Emperor awaited him.

"Well?" He sneered at the Grand Domestic.

“She fell off the seawall.” Maxentios replied solemnly. “And there’s a ship approaching, and it’s Norman.”

“Do what needs to be done to stop them.” The Emperor was so enraged, his words were eerily calm, “All of them.”

TO BE CONTINUED.

GLOSSARY OF TERMS

Augusta – Latin word for empress, borrowed word in Greek during this period to define that the empress was considered to be almost equal in power to the emperor.

Barbarian – Used to define anyone who was not Greek or Roman, but could often be derogatory in nature.

Boukoleon Palace – An Imperial residence of the Great Palace complex. Located immediately on Propontis (the Sea of Marmara).

Christ *Pantokrator* – An image of Christ in the Orthodox church that portrays him overseeing all. It is believed that a large mosaic of Christ *Pantokrator* is covered up by Muslim decorations in the Hagia Sophia, from when it was converted to a mosque post Ottoman takeover in 1453.

Clavii – Vertical stripes on clothing that run continuously from front to back over the shoulders. A common ornamentation in Roman fashion.

Dromon: A small and swift Byzantine naval boat.

East Sea – Period name for the Baltic Sea, as said by Germanic and Norse.

Euxine Sea – Period name for the Black Sea

Gate of the Spring – One of the gates of the Theodosian Land Walls. Currently known as the Gate of Selymbria in modern Istanbul.

Greece – The period Scandinavian term for the Eastern Roman Empire.

Greek(s) – Western and Northern Europeans often referred to the Eastern Romans as Greeks to differentiate them from the Holy Roman Empire, which they referred to as Romans. (The Romans referred to their counterparts as Germans.)

Hagia Sophia – Means "Holy Wisdom" in Greek. A large basilica in Constantinople that was commissioned by Justinian I. Still standing in modern Istanbul today after serving as a mosque during Ottoman times. Now a museum.

Hippodrome – Large, oblong arena in Constantinople used for horse and chariot racing. Parts still remain in modern Istanbul as a public park.

Kathisma – The Imperial balcony overlooking the Hippodrome. Directly accessible from the Great Palace.

Kyria – "Lady" in Greek.

Kyrie Eleison – "Lord, have mercy." Primarily a liturgical prayer and chant in both Orthodox and Latin services, can be used as a profane swear.

Megas Domestikos – Literally "Grand Domestic" in Greek. The commander of the land armies of Rome and immediate second-in-charge to the emperor.

Miklugaard – Old Norse name for Constantinople

Pallium – Tabard-like, heavily ornamented garment worn by Eastern Roman imperials.

Prinkípissa – "Princess" in Greek. In Anna's case, an honorary title.

Porphyrogénnētos - “Born into the Purple”, A title reserved for true princes and princesses of the blood born to the emperor and empress in the Porphyry Chamber who are direct Imperial heirs. Anna's son, Alexei, holds the title of prince because it was inherited from his father, who was born of a brother to the previous emperor, and therefore, not an Imperial heir. The current emperor is also not a *porphyrogénnētos,* but he took the throne by force.

Propontis – Period name for the Sea of Marmara

Rasshol – Period Norse for “asshole.”

Salvete omnes. – Latin for “Greetings, all.”

Scramasax – A type of large knife that was worn by men in the 5th to 11th century in Northern Europe.

Sudarium – A decorative, perfumed handkerchief or scarf common in Eastern Roman wardrobe.

Strigil – A curved metal bath implement used to scrape dirt and oil from the body. Used before soaps were available.

Valhalla – A hall in the Norse afterlife where one would go if they died in combat.

Varangoi – Greek plural form of Varangians.

Via Egnatia – A Roman road that stretches across the Greek peninsula from the Adriatic Sea to Constantinople.

Xylokerkos Gate - Also known as the Second Military Gate, is one of the gates of the Theodosian Land Walls. Now known as the Belgrade Gate in modern Istanbul.

ABOUT THE AUTHOR

Angela L. Costello had her first book "published" at the age of ten through the Young Authors Conference held at the University of South Florida. Now, she considers herself an industry professional geek who lives and works in Providence, Rhode Island. She's been infatuated with history and the classics since a young age and is currently pursuing studies in these fields at the University of Rhode Island. Holding a previous degree from the International Academy of Design in Tampa Bay where she grew up, Angela has a way of transforming her ideas creatively from pen to graphic and even fabric.

When she isn't at school, working in her costume shop, drawing, or apparently writing, you can find her at events for the Society for Creative Anachronism (SCA,) which inspired this book.

Doodle on this page.

Made in the USA
Charleston, SC
21 October 2012